"Do you rate me the same sort of brute as your stepfather?"

There was a taut silence before she answered. "From my observations you have a lot in common."

"Yes, I can see you might think that. After all, we are both men, which is what you really fear, isn't it?"

"I don't know what you mean."

"I mean that you are a coward, Robin Dale. I mean that you are afraid of men, of sex, of everything that makes you human. That's why there have been no lovers to mess up your tidy life. You were too damned scared."

"I haven't wanted a lover. It's got nothing to do with being scared. If I'd wanted one, I would have—"

"Reached out and taken one? As you did last night?" Guy finished for her.

She wanted to deny it. But the truth was she wanted Guy, and the strength of her desire both thrilled and appalled her. And now he knew it.

SOPHIE WESTON wrote and illustrated her first book—at the age of five. After university she decided on a career in international finance, which was tremendously stimulating and demanding, but it was not enough. Something was missing in her life, and that something turned out to be writing. These days her life is complete. She loves exciting travel and adventure yet hates to stray too long from her homey cottage in Chelsea, where she writes.

Books by Sophie Weston

These books may be available at your local bookseller.

Don't miss any of our special offers. Write to us at the following address for information on our newest releases.

Harlequin Reader Service
901 Fuhrmann Blvd., P.O. Box 1397, Buffalo, NY 14240
Canadian address: P.O. Box 2800, Postal Station A,
5170 Yonge St., Willowdale, Ont. M2N 6J3

SOPHIE WESTON

like enemies

Harlequin Books

TORONTO • NEW YORK • LONDON
AMSTERDAM • PARIS • SYDNEY • HAMBURG
STOCKHOLM • ATHENS • TOKYO • MILAN

Harlequin Presents first edition September 1986
ISBN 0-373-10918-0

Original hardcover edition published in 1986
by Mills & Boon Limited

CHAPTER ONE

'GUY GERRARD is an important man,' said Sally in a troubled voice. 'We can't afford to offend him, Robin.'

'I don't intend to offend him,' Robin Dale said tiredly, running her hands through her leaf-brown hair in a revealing gesture. 'I am just not going to do any more work for him.'

Sally Jackson bit her lip. 'Have you discussed it with Marina?'

'Marina, as you very well know, is sunning herself somewhere in the Tuscan Hills and is quite uncontactable. Until she telephones me I have no way of getting in touch with her.'

'But it's such a big step, Robin. After we worked so hard to get his contract.'

Robin shrugged slim shoulders, not answering. She knew it was a big step to take. Marina had left her in charge and had not expected that during her absence her second-in-command would dispatch her newest, most valued client. Robin kept telling herself that Guy Gerrard would not withdraw the offer of a contract to refurbish his company's London hotel simply because Marina Interiors were no longer willing to design his Mayfair home. But she lacked conviction, and Sally Jackson, Marina's personal assistant and trusted friend, knew it.

'What's one house more or less?' Robin said in spite of her inner doubts. 'We've got plenty of work apart from that.'

'Oh, come on, Robin, you know it's more than just another house. We've been half promised the Lambert

5

House Hotel. Marina's already tendered for it. You know she said Mr Gerrard was very impressed by her preliminary ideas. As he was for the designs of his own home, he told her.'

'*My* preliminary ideas,' Robin reminded her gently.

A faint frown crossed Sally's face. 'Does that make any difference?'

Robin sighed. 'Yes, I'm afraid it does. You see, *I'm* not prepared to do any more work for Mr Gerrard. Oh, Lambert House is different. It's owned by a public company of which Mr Gerrard just happens to be the Managing Director. He could be sacked tomorrow.' Her expression said that she wished he would be. 'I'll do the work there, if we get the contract. But I won't work personally for anyone who behaves as he has done.'

Sally sighed, studying the unusually drawn face in front of her. Normally, Robin Dale was vitally alive, sparkling with fun and energy. The sherry-brown eyes were frank, reflecting every mood. Usually they expressed a curiosity and zest for life which made her one of the most charming people Sally had ever encountered.

Today, though, was different. The charm, the liveliness, were doused as if someone had flung a bucket of water over her. In fact, Robin had been different since yesterday afternoon when Lamia Frizell, the new trainee, had announced that she did not want to go back to the Gerrard house in Hill Place and, when pressed for her reasons, had burst into panic-stricken tears.

Robin had taken her off to her sunny grey and lemon office to talk the matter over and no more was seen of Lamia. At six o'clock Robin had emerged to say that she had sent the girl home to work on another design project, and had looked, Sally thought in consternation, as if young Lamia had been beating her instead of weeping on her shoulder.

rawing board, running her long fingers idly along its
dge. She did not look at Sally. 'She didn't want to talk
bout it, you know. It happened two days ago and she
idn't tell any of us. It was just when Dick told her to
o back to Hill Place to see the carpenter that she got a
it excited about not wanting to go back.'

Sally said, 'Perhaps she's upset him somehow.'

'Oh, I should think she's done that,' Robin said drily.
I gather she turned him down flat and ran out of the
ouse.'

'Could she have misunderstood, do you think? I
nean she's very young . . .'

'And perfectly sensible.' Robin bent her head against
he drawing board, her brow heated where it touched
he cool paper. 'No, I don't think she misunderstood
im. She even blames herself. She says she hero-
worshipped him a bit; she was impressed. Well, it's easy
nough to imagine; the dashing international socialite
othering to be kind to an employee.' Robin's voice
ripped contempt. 'She says he's very attractive, too.
he thinks he probably got the wrong idea because she
vas a bit dazzled by him.'

'Well, perhaps she's right. If he thought she fancied
im, and he found her attractive, there would be
othing wrong in him doing something about it.' Sally
ave Robin a minatory look over the top of her
aborate spectacles. 'You're letting your own prejudices
n away with you. Not everybody is as violently anti-
en as you are.'

'I'm not anti-men,' Robin protested. They had had
s argument before. 'Some of my best friends are
n.'

Well, anti-sex then. You can't say that you ever get
olved. But you forget that everyone isn't the same as
. Lamia,' added Sally drily, thinking of the young
n in sports cars who waited for the trainee at night

Although at six o'clock Marina Interiors was
nominally closed for the day, everybody had still been
there. They were a small team still, in spite of the
success of the last eighteen months, and they were close
to each other. It was Dick Hadrian who had voiced
everyone's thoughts.

'You look as if you've been sandbagged, Robin.
What on earth has the child been up to?'

There had been a quick flash of fire in the brown gaze
as she turned to him. 'Why should you assume she's
been up to anything, Dick? Why are you so ready to say
it is her fault?'

He was taken aback by the quick retort but not
shaken from his easy-going composure.

'Because she looked the picture of guilt, my pet. I
gussed she'd been bumping into Guy Gerrard's Ming
vases and grinding them into the Aubusson. Was I
wrong?'

The fire died. Once again, Robin was pale and
strained, the pure oval of her face sharply etched by
tension, the eyes as dark as velvet under the level brows.
Whatever it was that was wrong, surmised Dick, it had
bitten very deep with Robin.

'You were wrong,' she said.

She looked round at them: steady, reliable Sally;
Dick; gentle Bill de la Croix; Tony Sefton, surprised out
of his habitual absent mindedness. She knew that
whatever decision she took would affect them all. Did
she have a right to take it without consulting them? Yet
at the same time could she bring herself to betray the
distraught girl's confidence?

Robin's hands clenched at her sides. For a few
moments, while she was pouring coffee for Lamia and
the girl, oblivious, was telling her story in harsh little
gasps, Robin had been brutally recalled to her eighteen-
year-old self. She had had no one to take her part, no

one in whom she dared confide until, in the end, the matter had been dragged into the spotlight and Robin had felt herself stripped and condemned by the very people who had failed to detect her victimisation.

Oh, they could do it so easily, she thought. The rich and powerful, the dominating, domineering male animal that took casually, as of right, whatever happened to strike it as desirable in the lesser members of the herd: she knew the type so well. She shuddered, remembering exactly how well she knew the type. Had she not been a piece of negligible plunder herself when, younger than Lamia now was, she had happened to attract the attention of a man without scruples?

She said quietly to the other members of the team, 'Mr Gerrard is taking—too close an interest.'

'But'—that was Tony, looking puzzled—'it's his home, Robin. He has to be there. He's bound to be interested.'

'In the outcome, perhaps,' she said swiftly. 'Not the progress.'

Tony was still bewildered. 'But if he wants to hurry up the plumbers, or whatever he's been doing, where's the harm in that?'

Robin looked down at her folded hands. This was difficult. 'None, intrinsically,' she allowed. 'Except that he's paying Marina Interiors to do it for him. And when he starts giving the workmen contradictory instructions to our own, he makes it impossible for all of us to do the job.'

She stood up, indicating clearly that she was not going to discuss the subject any further that night. They had to be content with what she had told them.

They did not question her, though they were plainly uneasy. It was Robin's talent that had, as Dick laughingly remarked, accelerated them to the point where they could breach the sound barrier. Since she

had joined them two years ago, the organisatio chaotic office had improved beyond recognitio same time as her novel designs had brought clients. So they trusted her.

Only Sally, the next day, sought a further e tion.

She said now, '*How* has he behaved, Robin? Y last night he was interfering too much. Are you throwing up the opportunity that Marina has v so hard for, out of pique?'

The beautiful face froze. 'What do you think?'

Sally said unhappily, 'I don't know what to t would never have expected you to react like this has the man *done*, in Heaven's name?'

Robin hesitated. Sally was entitled to an expla she knew. She made up her mind. 'Look, Sally, t for passing on to anyone else, right?'

Sally nodded.

'You know Lamia's been round at Gerrard every day this week? Well, so has he. Althoug us he would not be there.'

Sally looked at her in disbelief. 'Are you that he's been chatting up Lamia? *Guy Gerra*

Robin bit her lip. How well she remembere note of incredulity, bordering on scorn. It man as dynamic and attractive as that possibly be interested in an unsophisticated But Robin had met a man very like him w too young to protect herself, and she knev more than possible.

'He's gone a bit further than chatting said quietly. 'He's frightened her half out

Sally sat down heavily. 'But—can yc mean she might just be making it up.'

Robin winced. She remembered that not making it up, Sally.' She stood up a

and the prolonged social telephone calls during the day,
'certainly isn't.'

'Perhaps not.'

'So—it could be a personal thing with Guy Gerrard.
She led him on, she changed her mind, whatever.'
Sally's voice softened. 'You have no way of telling,
Robin. You can't condemn the man unheard.'

Robin spun round on her heel. 'Sally, she's *afraid* of
him.' Her voice cracked. 'I mean really afraid. You
should have seen her yesterday. She was almost
desperate not to go back. She talked about resigning—
and you know how serious she is about her career.'

Sally was shaken. Lamia was lively and very young
and, in Sally's view, a bit flighty but there was no doubt
about her commitment to her career. If she would
rather resign than face Guy Gerrard again then things
were bad indeed.

She said anxiously, 'You've still only heard one side
of the story.'

Robin's smile was twisted. 'I haven't even heard that.
She wouldn't tell me what happened. I think she's
ashamed, poor child. I more or less deduced what went
on and when I put it to her she got very upset.'

'Oh,' said Sally, impressed against her will.

'And as for the other things you suggested—did she
lead him on, change her mind too late, that sort of
thing: well, that's what everyone says on these
occasions. Lamia isn't denying it. In a court of law, no
jury in the country would convict.'

'So what makes you different?' asked Sally curiously.
'Because you've convicted him, haven't you, Robin?
Without even a token hearing.'

'Have I?' Robin was startled. 'I didn't think of it like
that.'

'No, so I see,' Sally agreed drily. 'But it's true,
nevertheless. You say yourself that you can't get any

sort of coherent story out of Lamia but you're prepared to give her the benefit of the doubt. Why not Guy Gerrard? Why take sides at all when you haven't got the full facts? It's pure prejudice; against an important client. And I don't see why.'

Robin flushed delicately. 'He's so much more experienced than Lamia,' she said, defending herself. 'He's older. He must have known what he was doing. He is a sophisticate . . .'

'And he's a man.' Sally looked at her gravely. 'That's the hub of the matter, isn't it, Robin? It's easy to think the worst of him because he's a man.'

There was a sharp silence while Robin strove with her feelings.

'Well, a man of that type,' she said at last, capitulating. She sank on to the lemon tapestry seat of her favourite Louis Quinze chair and pushed the hair wearily off her face. 'And whether he's truly to blame or not, you must see that it would be the height of cruelty to force Lamia to go back to that house.'

'Yes, I see that,' Sally agreed.

'So what else can we do but bow out gracefully? The whole thing is too advanced to pull anyone else into the project. Lamia did all the work.'

'On your designs. As you have just reminded me.'

Robin dismissed that with a wave of the hand. 'They're Lamia's workmen, the builders, the decorators . . .' She trailed off, staring at Sally. 'Are you suggesting that I finish it myself? That *I* take charge of the day to day work?'

Sally looked down, a small smile playing about the corners of her mouth. 'As you say, nobody else would qualify.'

'But I'm so busy. I can't be away from the office for hours at a stretch, particularly not while Marina is on holiday.'

'You could take your drawing board with you?' Sally suggested. 'Instal yourself in one of the attic rooms that they haven't started work on yet?' Sally knew the exact progress of every project at any time. 'I don't suppose he'd mind. Particularly not if he was getting your personal supervision.'

'But the office,' murmured Robin.

'It may have escaped your attention but we are well within walking distance of Hill Place. I could bring important things round to you. Say twice a day after I have opened the post. And there's always the telephone. Lamia says that is due to be connected this week.' Sally looked at her straightly. 'Inconvenient, I know. But isn't it worth the inconvenience for a couple of weeks to be helpful to an important client?'

Robin frowned. 'But I don't want to be helpful to him.'

'No, I know, you'd rather see him horse-whipped,' Sally sounded amused. 'You're not the arbiter of his morals, Robin. If you keep Lamia out of his orbit, you've done all you can reasonably be expected to do.'

'I suppose you're right,' Robin sighed. 'He ought to be taught a lesson but Marina Interiors is hardly in a position to do anything about that.'

Sally shook her head. 'Never mix business with pleasure. Particularly not when the pleasure is revenge.'

Robin gave a little choke of laughter. 'You're definitely right there. Oh damn, I suppose I shall have to go over there myself. And I particularly detest that sort of man.'

'That in itself is something I find rather intriguing,' Sally said casually, preparing to leave.

'Yes, well . . .' Robin was not to be drawn.

She knew quite well that her colleagues at Marina Interiors had first been astonished and then disbelieving about the limited extent of her social life. She inhabited an elegant eighth-floor flat in Kensington where she lived alone. If she was invited out to a reception or dinner party by a client she either went alone or was escorted by one of her fellow directors from Marina Interiors. In fact there was, quite clearly, no man in her life and she seemed bent on preserving the status quo. Men who showed any signs of being interested in her in other than a remotely friendly way, were rejected in no uncertain terms.

'She told me she didn't have affairs with colleagues,' Bill de la Croix had told Sally wryly when they were having a drink one evening after work.

Sally knew quite well that Robin's charm and liveliness had had an immediate impact on her soft-spoken companion and that he was in a fair way to having lost his heart. She patted his hand in silent sympathy.

'And she says she doesn't have affairs with clients because that's bad for business,' Bill went on. 'And she never goes out in the evening because she's always working; and all her friends are either women or married. So who's left?'

He had put much the same argument to Robin herself when he was urging her to spend a weekend with him at his sister's country cottage.

'Nobody's left, Bill,' Robin had told him quietly. 'That's the way I like it.'

'B-but why? You're young, you're unattached.' A thought struck him. 'You *are* unattached. There's no discarded husband lurking in the background?'

Robin shook her head.

'Then why?' Bill spread his hands in a comic gesture of incomprehension. 'It's a terrible waste of gorgeous material.'

She gave a little laugh at that, blushing faintly as he observed to his surprise. It always disconcerted him to be reminded how very low Robin rated her own attractions.

'I guess I'm just made that way,' she said evasively and changed the subject.

And that was what she always did whenever the matter was referred to again. Bill might sigh miserably, Sally might make critical comments, Marina could and did rant operatically against Robin immuring herself in work and turning her back on what Marina described as the real world. It made not the slightest difference. Robin would smile, agree, and refuse to talk about it. In the end it became accepted.

And now, Sally thought, it would be very interesting to see how Robin coped with daily proximity to a man who was not only as dynamic and hardworking as she was herself but had a considerable reputation for charm into the bargain. She obviously started out with a prejudice against him. Perhaps she even feared that her hitherto impregnable defences might be breached by the man. Sally was not an unkind girl but she was very fond of Bill de la Croix and it would give her a certain small satisfaction if Robin's self-sufficiency took a dent, quite apart from the fact that she thought it would be good for Robin herself.

Robin, walking down to Hill Place from Marina Interiors' pretty mews headquarters, entertained no such thoughts. She was not afraid of the effect that Guy Gerrard might have on her otherwise impervious heart. It never even occurred to her that he might have any effect at all.

Her whole feeling was one of impatience and reluctance. It was not that she thought that Gerrard would turn his dubious attention towards herself. For one thing, if he found the youthful Lamia, with her breathless voice and puppyish high spirits, attractive, he was unlikely to be drawn to Robin. For another, she was perfectly capable of registering twenty degrees of frost if he tried. No, it was more nebulous than that.

For one thing, she was out of sympathy with the project. To begin with Gerrard had simply bought the delapidated house in Hill Place and commissioned Marina to transform it from its existing disposition as a number of tatty offices, back into the family home for which it had originally been designed. Marina was given *carte blanche*. There were no specifications about size of rooms, number of bathrooms, not even where the kitchen and dining rooms should be. Gerrard had simply delegated the whole thing.

Robin had the impression that he was too busy to bother with it. It was that alone which had allowed Marina to persuade her to take it on. Normally when they were designing a private home, they worked very closely with the client. And Robin, having been savaged by just such a successful, polished, popular figure as Guy Gerrard, would not have accepted a diamond mine in return for such work. It was not that she was afraid of the type; not any more. She had faced what they could do to her and overcome it. It was simply that they filled her with distaste. And to design a house for someone to feel comfortable in, Robin knew that she could not afford to loathe them and everything they stood for.

So the fact that Guy Gerrard was now taking more than a passing interest in the reconstruction of his home gave Robin real professional problems. Without Lamia to act as a buffer between them, she would have to put a careful guard over her tongue. Though there was one faint ray of hope: Lamia had seemed to suggest that Gerrard had introduced a new lady into his life. If she were taking an interest in the house in Hill Place, reasoned Robin, then it might be possible to deal with her rather than direct with the unwelcome client.

And anyway, it could not go on for long. The structural work was done. Robin ran lightly up the shallow steps of the house, telling herself firmly that, though temporarily unpleasant, her professional dealings with Mr Gerrard would be of the shortest possible duration.

CHAPTER TWO

SLIGHTLY to Robin's surprise, and not at all to her taste, Guy Gerrard was waiting for her in one of the downstairs rooms. He called out to her before she had so much as shut the heavy oak door behind her. There was no mistaking the imperious note in his voice—this was a man who was used to being obeyed and would not brook resistance to his directions.

Trying hard not to let that tone of command reinforce her prejudice against the man, Robin obediently went into the room from which he had hailed her. Hearing her approach he swung round neatly from the window. Robin stopped dead.

But he is too young, she thought in confusion, staring at him. With his reputation, his achievements, she had expected a man not so far away from her stepfather's vintage. What she confronted was very different.

Where her stepfather had been paunchy and lined, this man was rangy, with a tanned sportsman's face. Her stepfather had moved ponderously, as if, she sometimes thought, he was bowing graciously to an invisible cheering populace. Guy Gerrard's movements were quick and precise and graceful, like a cat's. His dark hair was springy and curly, with just a touch of grey at the sides which, oddly, made his face look even more unexpectedly youthful. But the startling thing was the colour of his eyes. They were blue as the sun-warmed Mediterranean at the height of summer and lit with laughter. At the moment he was undoubtedly laughing at her openly.

18

Robin shook her head to clear it, transfixed by the intensity of that wicked laughter. 'Mr Gerrard?'

The graceful, silent stride had already brought him to her side. 'Miss Dale. Or is it Mrs Dale?'

She shrugged, removing her hand from his. 'Does it matter?'

He looked mischievous. 'Not very much these days. Mrs is no longer a clear indication of the married state. And Miss is certainly no guarantee that the lady is unattached. But as a matter of courtesy I would hate to address you by the wrong title.' His mouth quirked. 'I am told you already disapprove of me enough already.'

Now who had told him that, Robin thought in annoyance.

But she said, 'I don't take offence so easily, Mr Gerrard. And I am not in the business of disapproving of influential clients.'

She had meant to sound dignified and remote. All that she managed, at least to her own ears, was petulance. Guy Gerrard's look of amusement deepened.

'Oh *dear*. That does sound bad. I can see I shall have to work hard to redeem myself.'

'I am sure that it cannot matter to you what I think of you, Mr Gerrard,' she said coolly. 'What I think about your house is rather more to the point. I gather you have some changes you want to make to the original designs.'

He gave her a faintly puzzled look, as if he were unused to having his light-hearted remarks so summarily dealt with. That gave Robin a little satisfaction, but not much. She found herself wishing desperately that she did not sound so pompous.

Gerrard did not comment on her primness, however, merely saying, 'I would like to discuss one or two changes, that's all. I'm still paying for your expert advice and I'll take it.'

Robin put up her brows. They were rather too thick for a woman and sometimes made her look very fierce, but they were highly expressive.

'You must make whatever changes you want, Mr Gerrard. It is going to be your home so you're the only expert, in the last analysis.'

He gave an exaggerated sigh of relief. 'I'm glad that you're so reasonable, Miss Dale.' Robin noted, with an annoyance that she could not account for, that he had settled on the unmarried title. 'I was prepared for battle. They told me you would be very hostile to any changes. It is, after all, your work of art, I suppose.'

'And you have to live in it. I don't.' She frowned. 'Who told you I would be difficult?'

Guy Gerrard shrugged. 'Oh, everyone. Specifically, Marina Komsolova. Oh, and the child that was here before, the one with the pearls and the finishing school voice.'

Robin was so angry at this dismissive reference to Lamia that for a moment she could not say a word. He had frightened Lamia half out of her wits and nearly out of her job, and he could not even be bothered to remember her name. A desire to show the callous Mr Gerrard that in her eyes he was less than the common earthworm took hold of Robin. She did not, however, allow it to show.

'Well, let us hope they have both overrated my ferocity,' she said drily, giving him a charming and utterly false smile. 'Do you have a list of the changes?'

The sea blue eyes were thoughtful. 'I've made a note of them and had my secretary type it out.' His tone was equable. 'I thought you might study them at your leisure today and then perhaps we could have dinner and discuss it.'

Robin's every instinct was to say no, unequivocally and at once. Only the suspicion that that was exactly what Guy Gerrard expected and was, indeed, banking on, gave her pause.

'Today?' she demurred.

She caught a quick flash of surprise before the heavy lids masked his eyes and felt a brief triumph.

'I travel a lot. I'm afraid I can't say when I'll next be in London. Tonight would be best.'

He was quite charming but quite firm. She could see why he was the managing director of a successful public company. She set her teeth and refused to be charmed.

'It doesn't give me a great deal of time to do justice to your suggestions,' she said. 'But that, of course, is your choice.'

Guy Gerrard gave her a curious look. 'No objections to this late alteration in your plans for the evening? You're happy to let me mess up your arrangements?'

Robin pretended to consider that. 'I wouldn't say happy, no.'

'But you nevertheless agree?' There was an odd note in his voice.

'Mr Gerrard,' said Robin softly, 'did you think for a moment I would not agree? Come, come, you must be used to being able to buy exactly what you want by now, whether it's a house in Mayfair or an evening of an interior decorator's time.'

He winced. 'Ouch, you hit hard, Miss Dale. I see what Marina meant. I'm sorry if I sounded a bit peremptory but I really am pressed for time at the moment. If it upsets your date for the evening, bring him along, too.'

Robin was tempted. She did not want to have to spend several hours sitting across a table from Guy Gerrard with no one else to share the attention of that perceptive gaze. But there were only the people from the office to ask and she did not think the tension would be alleviated by the presence of Bill de la Croix, hurt but hopeful, or the ever-inquisitive Dick.

So she inclined her head graciously and declined. Guy Gerrard had a mobile face that could register whatever emotion he chose. Now he presented a pantomime of comic respect.

'You must have a very understanding boyfriend, Miss Dale, if he lets you stand him up at less than a day's notice.'

She ignored the implied question. 'I am first, last and always a career woman, Mr Gerrard. My friends know that.'

'They know they take second place to your professional clients?' he sounded astonished.

'They don't always have to,' Robin retorted.

His eyes twinkled. 'Only when the client is outrageously demanding?'

She refused to smile back at him. 'You said that, Mr Gerrard, I did not.'

'And the client is always right,' he observed softly.

Robin thought she detected scorn in the cool tones and masked her surging dislike only with difficulty. 'Not always, Mr Gerrard. At least not in my opinion. But the client always gets what he wants, whether he's right or not.'

The gold-flecked eyes met his in unspoken challenge. For a moment his expression was quite unreadable. Then one eloquent eyebrow flew up and he was full of mockery.

'I shall bear that in mind in all our dealings, Miss Dale.' The eyes flickered over her once, comprehensively, and came to rest on her mouth. Robin could no more have prevented the blood from staining her pale cheeks than she could have stopped herself taking one involuntary half pace backward as he advanced. His smile grew. 'I shall look forward to this evening,' he told her lightly.

And was gone.

After that, Robin did not have a good day. If there had been a telephone installed in the house she would have rung his office and cancelled the arrangement. The thought of Sally's amusement, however, if she asked her to take any such message was more than she could bear. So there was nothing to do but let it stand.

She did not even know how or where he would meet her. It occurred to her to go home to her flat and tell the porter not to let any importunate visitors come up. But she quickly discarded the idea. Guy Gerrard was quite capable of tracking her to her home and of circumventing the porter if he chose. No, it was safer to stay at the mews cottage that was the headquarters of Marina Interiors and keep Gerrard off her private territory.

Robin made the rounds of the house with grim conscientiousness, files in hand. She had not done such work for over a year. Marina thought it better to delegate the practical work to juniors and concentrate Robin's talents and time exclusively on designing. Robin had therefore rather forgotten how much she enjoyed the practical side of the job.

She found that Lamia had done a reasonably efficient job. There were one or two delays that she had not noted and one quite serious patch of damp that had appeared on the top floor landing that she had not given the builders instructions about but otherwise everything seemed in satisfactory order. Guy Gerrard would have had no cause to complain about her.

Robin set herself up on the top floor after she had done her rounds and talked to all the tradesmen at work on the house. The old attic was not very warm but that did not matter on this bright summer day. It had two distinct advantages—plenty of light and an absolute absence of any builders' clutter. Robin set up her easel and folding chair on the stripped floorboards and went to work.

There was no electricity in the house as yet and all the workmen had brought themselves flasks of tea or coffee. When Sally arrived with the morning's post she, too, was bearing a thermos flask of black coffee. Robin recieved her rapturously.

'I was wondering how long I could last without,' she confessed, pouring the steaming black liquid into the two cap cups with which the thermos was furnished.

'Lamia warned me. Though of course I knew that the rewiring wasn't completed,' Sally told her tranquilly, taking up a perch on the wooden window seat.

'So did I,' agreed Robin ruefully. 'I *knew* it, from the progress report in the file, but I just didn't make the connection to deducing that that meant no electric kettle and no coffee.'

Sally looked at the forlorn kettle in the corner of the room and grinned. 'So I see.'

'I know. I know. I'm a fool.' Robin flung up her hands in mock surrender.

'Not according to your fan club. A genius maybe. And geniuses can't be expected to grapple with the small things of life like coffee.'

'Coffee,' said Robin with feeling, 'is not a small thing.' They sipped in companionable silence for a moment and then she said curiously, 'What fan club?'

Sally shrugged. 'Marina. The boys. The Salazar Corporation.'

Robin frowned a little. 'But not you?'

'No. Not me.' Sally gave her a level look. 'Maybe it's because I'm not creative. I don't think your attainments in design outweigh the arid life you lead. But you know that.'

'You've never made any secret of it,' Robin agreed wryly.

When she had first come to work for Marina Komsolova she had thought that Sally was definitely hostile, even an enemy. Over the months they had come to respect each other's work and even, within certain limits, like each other. But Sally, the offspring of a large and cheerful family who saw her brothers and sisters and nieces and nephews regularly, could not disguise the fact that she found Robin's solitary life faintly suspect. And, of course, there was Bill, as Robin had found out.

Sally shrugged. 'It's none of my business what you do with your life.'

'No,' Robin agreed.

Sally shot her a quick look. 'But isn't it difficult designing houses—-I mean real homes for people, like this one—when you're so out of touch?'

'I'm not out of touch with the materials that are available. I know about wallpapers and carpets and furniture,' said Robin. 'That's what they pay me for. So they don't have to do their own research and spend time on their own buying trips. They don't pay me to feel for them.'

'Which is just as well, as you haven't got a gramme of feeling in your whole body,' said Sally, on a flash of irritation. Then, 'No, I shouldn't have said that. I apologise.'

'Why? If it's what you think you're perfectly entitled to say it. I wouldn't disagree with you, either.'

Sally stared at her.

'About feeling,' Robin elaborated. 'I should think I'm about as unfeeling as it is possible to get. I certainly hope so.'

Sally shook her head, as if not believing what she heard.

'B-but why, Robin?'

Robin smiled crookedly. 'I did all my feeling when I was an adolescent. I positively weltered in it. If I hadn't broken out of it—with the help I may say of an old friend who knew the dangers of emotionalism—I'd probably have collapsed or gone mad. Anyway, these days I keep my life on an even keel. I should think,' she added reflectively, 'that I used up all my store of feelings before I was twenty.'

Sally, instead of looking horrified, as Robin had half expected, seemed sympathetic.

'Love affair go wrong?' she asked, settling down for a comfortable exchange of confidences.

But that was something Robin certainly did not want. She had not confided in anyone, not when she was eighteen and not since. Like Lamia, she had been ashamed. She had wanted to put it all behind her. It was possible, even probable, that her godfather Felix Lamont knew roughly what had happened, but nobody else did. Or rather nobody else knew the full sum; a number of people who had played their part at the time knew some of it. But she had not seen them for a long time. She had never talked about it to them.

So she shook her head. 'Not a love affair.'

Sally frowned, as if she were trying to work out some peculiarly knotty clue in a crossword puzzle. 'Then why this antipathy to men?'

'I've told you,' Robin said patiently. 'I'm not antipathetic to men. I just don't want my life messed up by anyone, man or woman. I don't want anyone getting too close.'

'B-but——'

'You're going to say that I could have more of a—er—fulfilled life without people getting too close.' Robin pushed her hands through her hair a little wearily. 'Maybe you're right. I know other people seem to hop in and out of love affairs without doing themselves or anyone else any damage. Well, look at Marina. She's hardly celibate but she's perfectly happy

and so are her lovers. The trouble is, I am just not that
sort of temperament.'

'No,' Sally agreed slowly. 'I can see that.'

'So it's much easier not to get involved in the first
place.'

There was a pause. Then Sally said, 'Do you know
what I think? I think you haven't exhausted your
capacity for feeling at all. I think it's all still there,
battened down. I think you're *afraid* of getting involved
with anyone in case you can't control it.'

She put down her coffee cup and stood up. Robin
said nothing.

'Well, it's up to you, of course. You know what you
want. But *I* think you'd better watch out, Robin. You
can't suppress your own nature for ever. And you know
what happens to people under pressure. You could be
heading for a big explosion.'

She gathered up her bag, and the letters they had
read and agreed an answer to, and left the attic quietly.

For the rest of the day Robin worked hard at putting
Sally's words out of her mind. They had given her a
nasty little shock, as if Sally was reminding her of
something she herself already suspected. It was a long
time since she had seriously thought about the present
tenor of her life and, at Sally's prompting, she found
she could not put it out of her head. And she did not
like it.

She was safe, she kept telling herself. She was
adequately clothed and fed, more than adequately
housed and employed in a job at which she was
outstanding. She gave a bitter little smile. It was not a
job she had been trained to do, but it was one for which
she had a natural talent, as her godfather had helped her
discover, and she knew without false modesty that she
was one of the best interior designers in London.

So why this feeling of restlessness, of dissatisfaction,

even? Her life was everything she thought she wanted: without the ties that had nearly strangled her when she was eighteen, without responsibilities for anyone but herself, without that dangerous exposure to emotion that Robin had learned to fear.

And yet today, between them, Sally Jackson and Guy Gerrard had made her feel uncertain, as if the perfect life that she had so carefully devised and pursued was, at bottom, unfulfilling. It was ridiculous. She began to leaf through her file and Guy Gerrard's suggested changes with a vigour bordering on impatience.

When Sally returned at four with more post and a flask of tea she also brought a message from Guy Gerrard.

'Or rather his secretary,' she corrected conscientiously. 'She said he would pick you up at the office at seven.' She gave Robin a curious look. 'A night on the town, for once?'

Robin shook her head. 'No, he wants to talk about the house and can't make any other time.'

Sally hesitated. 'You aren't planning on doing anything silly, are you?'

Robin raised her eyebrows. 'Silly?'

'Like taking him to task over Lamia.'

'We haven't discussed Lamia,' Robin said with truth.

'Or teaching him a lesson?'

Robin's long gold-tipped lashes veiled her eyes. 'That depends,' she said slowly.

Sally looked alarmed. 'Depends on what?'

'How he behaves, of course.' Robin gave her a brilliant smile, full of mischief; reluctantly Sally found herself smiling back. 'There's quite a big score against him. But I'm not judge and jury, as you said yourself and it's none of my business. Provided he stays businesslike, I shall be as good as gold, just as you want.'

Sally groaned. 'Oh lord, that sounds ominous.'

Robin shook her warm brown head, laughing. 'Not at all. I am reassuring you.'

'You are?' Sally's aspect was one of profound misgiving. 'What do you mean by businesslike? And what happens if he isn't?'

'Businesslike——' Robin considered it, head on one side, 'means talking about the transaction in hand and nothing else. If he tries any of the famous charm, I shall crunch him.'

Sally shuddered. 'I've seen you. The poor man has my sympathy. He doesn't know what he's getting into.'

Robin thought about that. He had said that he knew she already disapproved of him. He thought it was rather funny, as far as she could judge.

'He knows,' she said, mouth tightening.

Sally's eyes widened. 'Robin you haven't already—I mean—you don't know him of old, or anything do you?'

Marina had once let slip that Robin's past was not only a taboo subject but had also been tumultuous. If Guy Gerrard was an old lover, Sally could not bear to think how Robin might react during a whole evening in his company. She was very sure that Marina Interiors would not have a contract with Mr Gerrard at the end of it. She looked at the other woman anxiously.

'I have never met him before today,' Robin said precisely, her lips curling in distaste. 'And though I didn't take to him, I was perfectly polite, so you can stop hopping from foot to foot. And I have every intention of staying polite . . .'

'Unless?' Sally prompted, with a sinking heart, noting the glitter in the usually soft amber eyes.

Robin gave her a little, half-shamefaced smile. 'Yes, of course, unless. Unless he tries to pull the same stunt with me that he tried on Lamia. Whatever it was.' The

rounded chin lifted. 'In which case,' Robin said softly,
'I shall go for the jugular and dashing Mr Gerrard will
wish he had never met either of us.'

The dashing Mr Gerrard, however, showed no signs
of doing any such thing when he arrived at the office to
collect Robin later that evening. It was considerably
later than seven o'clock for which he apologised
formally, but as if his mind were really somewhere else.
He looked, thought Robin with a twinge of compassion
that surprised her, tired to the point of exhaustion. She
was annoyed with herself. She did not want to feel any
sympathy for this dictatorial client.

'We've got a table booked at the Four Horsemen,' he
told her. 'Do you know it?'

'I've never heard of it,' Robin confessed.

He smiled. 'I'm not surprised. It's hardly fashionable.
But it's convenient and there's a garden where we can
sit and have a drink.' He ran a hand through his
springy hair. 'It's too hot and sticky to stay in London
at all really. I should have taken you somewhere out
along the river. Windsor maybe. But I didn't know
what time my meeting would finish.'

'You don't have to apologise,' Robin said composedly. 'I wasn't expecting . . .' She broke off, realising
that what she had been about to say was hardly
complimentary.

'To enjoy yourself?' Guy Gerrard supplied softly.
'No, you made that very clear earlier.'

He swung the big Mercedes out of the mews with the
ease of long practice. The car moved smoothly, silently,
the engine no more than a faint background purr.
Robin felt her heart began to beat hard, for no reason
that she could name, and had a horrible feeling that he
could hear it.

She decided that attack was the best form of defence.

'I didn't think you had asked me out to enjoy myself,

Mr Gerrard. I thought you had commanded my company in order to give me instructions about the house.'

He pulled a face. 'That sounds very inconsiderate of me.' He paused and added with unconcealed amusement, 'And very rash.'

Robin cast him a look of dislike and drummed her fingers on the soft leather of her shoulder bag. 'Rash? Hardly, Mr Gerrard. You are paying, after all.'

'I am indeed,' he said ruefully. 'Are you going to snipe at me all evening, Miss Dale, or will you count yourself satisfied if I apologise prettily now?'

Robin was tempted to respond to the almost irresistible gleam of fun in the azure eyes. But she had had a disturbing day, passing her lifestyle under review, and she was still profoundly shaken by Lamia's distress. So she shrugged, not answering.

'You're not very gracious,' he complained. His tone was still light but there was a hint of steel there. He was obviously not used to having his overtures rejected, thought Robin.

'I am sorry,' she said insincerely.

'I doubt it,' he returned. 'What do you want, Miss Dale? I can't do any more than apologise.'

It was on the tip of her tongue to ask him whether he had apologised to Lamia but she decided against it. He had no idea that she knew about that little episode.

She said crisply, 'Don't be ridiculous, Mr Gerrard. You don't have to apologise for taking me out to dinner. If it was the only time you had available, then it was quite understandable. But as I am sure that you have other calls on that time—as I certainly have—let us not prolong it unneccessarily.'

Oh lord, there she went again, sounding as prim and pompous as an ageing spinster in a farce. Guy Gerrard obviously thought so, too. He gave her a quick, unsmiling look, as if he were surprised, and all vestige of that famous charm evaporated.

'As you wish,' he said and closed his lips in a firm line that suddenly made him look a good deal more formidable than Robin, who knew and respected his reputation in the professional field, would have believed possible.

For the first time, and too late, she began to wonder whether, in giving rein to her private prejudices in her dealings with Guy Gerrard, she had issued a challenge which she would have difficulty in maintaining. She had not felt fear of another person for ten years. At eighteen she had vowed that no man was going to frighten her again. Dimly she perceived that this man, if he chose to exert himself, could blow that resolution and excellent record to pieces.

CHAPTER THREE

THE rest of the journey was accomplished in silence. That might have been due to the change in his mood. It might equally well have been attributable to the complexity of their route.

Slightly to Robin's surprise, he did not take her to one of the select nightspots that he was said to patronise in the West End. When he had said that the restaurant was not fashionable she had assumed him to mean that it had not yet been discovered by the smart set among which he normally moved. She had not expected to be taken by backstreets which he obviously knew with long familiarity, into a slightly raffish area of Chelsea.

He took the car into a narrow street, hardly more than an alley, and swung it to a halt outside a dimly lit building at the end of a high white wall. Above the wall Robin could make out lilac blossom and the tops of trees and from behind it came the subdued buzz of conversation. Guy Gerrard got out just as a white painted door opened and a small dark man appeared.

The engine was still running as he came round to the passenger door to help her out. Robin looked questioningly as she obeyed the imperative hand.

'As you see this is not an ideal area to park a car. Leo does it for me.'

And indeed the other man, grinning hugely, was already sliding behind the wheel. Guy put a hand under her elbow.

'I hope you don't consider a drink before dinner too much of a waste of time, Miss Dale,' he said coolly. 'I've had a tough day and I need a Scotch.'

Without waiting for her reply he led her through the small door and into a charming garden, full of honeysuckle and jasmine and trees, with even a small patch of green velvet lawn where sparrows were picking energetically at crumbs. There were perhaps half a dozen other people there.

A man in a blazer hurried forward. 'Signor Gerrard. When Maria told me you had booked a table I was overjoyed. We have not seen you for so long. It is a great pleasure. You are in your house, yes?'

'Giulio!' It was a greeting of undisguised pleasure. Robin looked at him curiously as he shook the other warmly by the hand. 'You're quite right, it's been too long.'

'Ah, it is because you live all the time in aeroplanes.'

'Too true,' Gerrard said with feeling. 'I've had more meals in mid air than on dry land this last month.'

Giulio clucked disapprovingly. 'Jet-lag destroys the palate. And I have some very special wine for you this evening. From Calabria. From my cousin.'

Guy Gerrard flung back his head and gave a shout of laughter.

'You don't change, Giulio.' He aimed a mock punch at his chest, still grinning. 'All right I'll buy it. We'll have a bottle of the cousin's vintage with our meal. And if it poisons Miss Dale, I will sue you. But now we want the menu and an aperitif. In fact I want Scotch. Miss Dale?'

Robin shook her head slightly. She was relieved to see that his mood had apparently lightened again but she was still sure that she needed to keep her wits about her.

'I'd like orange juice please.'

Giulio beamed at her. 'But certainly, certainly. My wife will squeeze some fresh juice for you at once, *bellissima signorina*.'

He bustled away and Guy Gerrard led her to a wooden seat round the trunk of a sycamore. He was drawing a slim cigarette from a silver case.

'I'm sorry. Do you smoke?'

'No, thank you.'

The blue eyes swept over her mockingly. 'You really have none of the vices, do you Miss Dale?'

He plumped the cushions up for her courteously and waited for her to seat herself before joining her on the bench and applying a thin flame to the tip of his cigarette. Then he inhaled luxuriously and leaned back, resting his dark head against the bole of the tree. There was a long pause.

'I hope the meal will be edible,' he murmured disconcertingly, at last.

Robin, who had sat tensely waiting for hostilities to be resumed, jumped.

'Isn't it usually?'

The long mouth curled in a reminiscent smile. 'The quality of the food is best described as variable. It all depends on the mood of the chef who is Giulio's brother. And as Giulio once told me, they are a very sensitive family.'

Robin was surprised at this sign of normal humanity. She would have judged Guy Gerrard as a man who insisted on the best of everything, for which he was well able to pay, and who would be impatient of anything inferior. She simply could not equate him with this amused tolerance for temperamental chefs in unfashionable restaurants.

'You've been coming here a long time?' she hazarded, trying to unfold the mystery.

'Years. Ever since I first came to London. When I came down from Cambridge I shared a flat with a couple of friends just round the corner. We used to come here all the time because it was cheap. And then we found out that when Filippo's wooing was going well or he had managed to avoid the taxman, the food was superb.'

Robin laughed. 'But these successes don't come often?'

He shook his head mournfully, his eyes dancing. 'Not often enough for Filippo to move on to the West End or to make this place more than moderately successful.'

'Why is it called the Four Horsemen?' Robin asked idly.

'Oh, that was a joke. When Giulio took it over, we'd been coming here for about a year and we knew all about Filippo's moods. He bought out the old boy who used to run it and said he wanted to change the name to reflect that. A sort of superstition, I suppose. Anyway, we suggested, Phil, Lionel and I, that they ought to call it Apocalypse because the food could be such a disaster.' He laughed, remembering. 'Filippo was so furious that he refused to cook at all and Maria had to take over for the rest of the evening. But in the end Giulio took our suggestion, though he modified it a bit to pacify Filippo.'

'I see.' Robin was amused. 'The Four Horsemen of the Apocalypse. Yes, it's not a very encouraging title for a restaurant.'

'But eminently honest,' Gerrard told her solemnly, 'a true and fair description if ever I heard one.'

She found herself warming to him, in spite of herself. This enjoyment of the ridiculous was very attractive; the more so for being unexpected.

She said abruptly, 'Why did you bring me here?'

At once the laughter died out of his face.

'It's nothing to do with you, Miss Dale. Don't worry, I'm not trying to insult you with second rate food. It is just that I wanted to come myself. I have had a hellish day on top of a bad month and I just wanted to relax somewhere peaceful and friendly. To forget for a while that I ever grew out of being the lad from the top floor flat on the corner. Can you understand that?'

She considered him thoughtfully. 'You mean luxury gets oppressive?'

He gave a crack of laughter. 'If it were only the luxury . . .'

'Then what?'

He drew again on the cigarette, his eyes darkening. Although he was looking directly at her, Robin had the feeling he was seeing something or someone very different which gave him no pleasure at all.

'It's tough being the head of a firm, the head of a family. People expect you to be able to solve all their problems, do you know that, Miss Dale? Because of the little bit of authority you have over their working lives, people expect you to have absolute knowledge of and responsibility for every other aspect of their existence. And within the family it's the same but worse.' He drew a little breath and then his eyes came back to her, seeing her again. 'I'm sorry, I'm not making much sense, am I? You don't know what I'm talking about and God forbid that you ever should.'

Robin sensed that there was something disturbing Guy Gerrard, in spite of his casual manner, that had shaken him to his foundations. She was puzzled. But she was also strangely moved, as if he were an old friend that she had known and loved for years, instead of a new and not-much-liked acquaintance.

She said, surprising herself, 'If there is anything I can do . . .?'

He gave her a quick, astonished look. Robin was already regretting the impulsive offer. He must think she was mad, a stranger, an employee after a fashion, inviting herself into his private life. She blushed and began to stammer a retraction just as Giulio returned with their drinks.

They did not refer to the subject again. For one thing Giulio, who plainly regarded Guy Gerrard as an old friend, did not leave them alone for more than ten minutes throughout the rest of the evening. For another Gerrard himself firmly changed the subject. Robin was grateful for it. She had been getting dangerously out of her depth for a few moments. It was a relief to return to the shallows where she was in control again.

She even enjoyed herself. Guy Gerrard was intelligent and widely travelled. He had read too much and seen too much to be dull and he was exerting himself to amuse her. He kept her in a ripple of laughter throughout the meal.

It was only when he was paying the bill and they were rising to go that she realised that, though they had skirted the subject a hundred times, they had reached no conclusions on the changes he proposed for his house. She said so, ruefully.

'Would it be easier if I put my thoughts on paper to you in the post?' she offered.

His eyes flickered, but he was smiling charmingly.

'Oh, it would be a pity to waste the rapport we have so unexpectedly built up this evening, don't you think? It would be better if you came back to my *pied à terre* to discuss it. I'll give you a brandy and we can go through the list quite quickly. I'll drive you home afterwards, of course.'

Robin hesitated. There was something more to the invitation than met the eye she was sure and yet it seemed silly to be suspicious. She did not for a moment believe he was bent on seducing her. She was no Lamia and anyway, though he had been a cordial host, he had shown no signs of overwhelming attraction to her during the meal. But nevertheless there was something there in an undercurrent to the smooth voice.

'I don't think . . .' she began but he interrupted.

'Oh come, Miss Dale, didn't you tell me that the customer is always right? And I'm leaving for Warsaw tomorrow for ten days. I'd like to get this cleared up before I go.'

In the face of so eminently reasonable an argument, Robin found she had nothing to say. It was not even late, since they had dined almost as soon as they arrived at the restaurant, and she could not honestly say she was tired. She gave a shrug.

'Very well.' It was her best cool tone, highly successful at repelling the over-ardent. 'As you also told me this afternoon, as I recall Mr Gerrard, you are paying handsomely for the privilege.'

His brows contracted swiftly in a savage frown. For a moment Robin thought she had gone too far and he would tell her to get out of his sight and take her portfolio and Marina Interiors' contract with her. And then, just as suddenly, the heavy lids veiled his eyes, and he was smiling gently.

'You are a bundle of contradictions, Miss Dale. Of course, all women are contrary creatures but you take it to extreme lengths.'

Robin bristled. 'An interesting specimen, in fact, Mr Gerrard?' she asked sweetly.

He held her chair for her to rise.

'Fascinating,' he told her coolly. 'And no doubt one that will repay study.'

Robin was still mulling over this oblique remark when they reached his flat. She forgot the vague sense of threat as she looked about her with interest. This was much more the setting she would have expected for him than an unfashionable restaurant in a back street.

The flat was in one of the prestige blocks where she had, over the years, done a good deal of work. The deeply carpeted hallway, with its antique gilded mirrors and discreet, uniformed porters also spoke, softly but unmistakably, of wealth. A small fountain played in the centre of the marble entrance hall, surrounded by palms and ivies in heavy stone pots. As they arrived a party was leaving, the women in bright gowns and furs, the men in dinner jackets, sweeping past the porter, who held the door for them, with the obliviousness of the very rich. Robin felt a flutter of dislike that was pure instinct and quelled it firmly. These were, after all, the sort of people from whom Marina Interiors made a not inconsiderable living.

Guy Gerrard had been talking to the porter in a low voice. Robin caught sight of notes changing hands, saw the porter nod and turn away.

'He's parking my car,' he told her, strolling over to her. 'They've got an underground car park here which is a miracle of packing. It takes ages to put a car away or get it out again, but at least it's out of the rain and away from the vandals.' He gave her that irresistible boyish grin. 'There must be more Rolls Royces to the square inch down there than tourists in Trafalgar Square.'

He took a key out of his pocket, unlocked the lift and ushered her inside. It rose in expensive silence to the top floor, Robin noted.

'Do you need a key to use every lift, or just this one?'

'That is astute of you,' he approved. 'Just this one. This is the only one that goes to the penthouse.' He leered at her. 'So you won't be able to get away from me without the key.'

Robin gave him a level look from cool sherry coloured eyes.

'I have no doubt there are stairs,' she said composedly. 'The fire regulations would require it.'

He groaned, clutching a hand to his head in mock dramatics.

'Discovered. And I thought I would have you at my mercy to do with as I pleased.'

The lift stopped with a whisper of machinery. The doors opened silently and Robin got out.

'You wouldn't have had that anyway,' she told him gently. 'Fire escape or no fire escape.'

Gerrard laughed. 'No, I believe you.'

She thought of Lamia and her lips tightened. 'I'm twenty-eight, Mr Gerrard, not a trembling adolescent. If people try to seduce me, I fight fire with fire.'

The lift opened directly into the sitting room. He followed her out and the doors closed behind him. Robin heard the machine glide away.

He was looking at her, an unreadable expression in his face. 'Now what does that sibylline remark mean?' he wondered. 'It almost sounds like a challenge.'

Robin shrugged one shoulder. 'A simple statement of intent. I wouldn't want you to be misled, Mr Gerrard.'

There was a good deal of amusement in his eyes. 'You really don't have much of an opinion of me, do you, Miss Dale?' he said drily. 'You keep telling me with admirable docility that the customer is always right but, not too far underneath, you think I'm a bit of a bounder who you would really much rather have nothing to do with.'

Robin gasped. This was plain speaking which outmatched her own with a vengeance. She did not know what to say. She knew she was blushing and cursed her fair, revealing skin for the fact that he could not fail to see it. He would probably interpret it as guilt, too, which was infuriating. She lifted her chin and glared at him.

'You know,' he said meditatively, 'I am strongly tempted to do something about that.'

'About what? My disapproval—that you think you can detect?' she asked disdainfully.

'No, not that. I don't tilt at windmills. About *that*,' he said, pinching her chin. 'The feminine defiance.'

Robin's eyes flickered and she took an involuntary step backwards. He gave an unamused laugh, suddenly looking tired.

'Oh, don't worry, Miss Dale. I'm no rapist, especially after a hard day. And delicious though it would undoubtedly be to give you some of your own back, I can't even summon the energy to give you a good ticking off. Though undoubtedly Marina ought to do something to stop you going round savaging her clients. Still, it's no concern of mine. Let me get you a brandy, agree the modifications to the house and then I'll get you home.' He gave her a wintry smile. 'And you can stop struggling to be polite to me, Miss Dale. I don't wilt from a little honest hostility, however ill-judged.'

He left her then, presumably to get the drink he had promised her, and Robin sank down into a deep chintz-covered sofa, feeling more than a little foolish.

Guy Gerrard came back almost immediately bearing a wooden tray on which reposed a decanter half full of walnut-brown liquid and two balloon-shaped glasses. He put them down on a chunky glass table and then, unexpectedly, went to a fitting on the wall and lowered the lights. Robin stiffened.

He brought a glass of brandy over to her saying, 'The lights are atrocious. They're on some sort of time switch. It's supposed to be an anti-burglar device. I suppose it may be effective but it does mean that you get home late at night and walk into neon illumina-tions.'

She said warily.

'Why don't you change them then?'

He laughed. 'Because, however arrogant you may think I am, Miss Dale, I don't go rearranging other people's domestic fittings when they lend me their flats.'

'Oh, I see.' She flushed, aware of being wrong-footed again. She was almost certain that he had done that deliberately. 'You don't own this place then?'

He looked round disparagingly at the pale furnishings, the stark lines of the glass tables and the fierce charcoal drawings on the walls.

'If you think I would be happy in this sort of set up then I'm amazed you managed to design me the home I wanted,' he remarked. 'It belongs to a friend of mine who's an actress. She has a different persona for every country. When in London, she's into cool Nordic sophistication.' He sounded amused, affectionate. 'I think she even has her hair tinted to go with it.'

'You relieve my mind,' Robin said drily and when he looked a question at her added sweetly, 'I was wondering whether I'd have to change the entire colour scheme of the house.' She pulled the portfolio from under her arm. 'Shall we begin?'

He was easy to deal with. His ideas were clear and he expressed them concisely. He was also perfectly practical and willing to compromise where it was clear that his ideas would cause an enormous increase in the time it would take to finish the house or in the overall expense. Robin was impressed.

At last she sat back on the sofa with a small sigh of satisfaction and sipped her hitherto untouched brandy, feeling quite in charity with him.

'I wish every client was as easy to deal with,' she told him.

He was leaning forward to pour himself more brandy but at that he looked over his shoulder at her, brows raised.

'You're not dismayed by the length of the list?'

She shook her head, smiling. 'Not at all. I have a list of my own of things to check and confirm which is five times the length of yours.'

'And most clients want even more?' he sounded appalled.

'Most clients don't know *what* they want,' Robin told him frankly. 'Quite often that's why they employ an interior decorator in the first place. Until you show them drawings they don't know what they don't want either. And then they have second, third, fourth and fifth thoughts . . .' She chuckled. 'I sometimes wonder whether they don't employ me to provide a little mental discipline.'

Guy Gerrard laughed softly. 'Well you have the resolution, I can see that.' He sank back into his corner of the deep sofa and considered her over the top of his brandy glass. 'Resolution, intelligence, a sense of fun, charm when you choose to use it——' he paused and then said with great deliberation, '—and poisonous prickles.'

Robin looked down at the brandy in her glass, prey to a mass of contradictory emotions. On the one hand she felt indignant, offended. Yet she could see that her demeanour this evening had given him every reason to think her a prickly character. On the other hand she felt oddly regretful, as if she knew that what he said was true, not just of her attitude to himself but to all men; and that it was too late to change it.

'Nothing to say?' he prompted softly.

She gave a small, sad smile, not answering. Her throat felt tight, almost as if she wanted to cry which was, of course, ridiculous.

He said, goading her, 'The customer is always right? Even when he insults you?'

Robin put down her glass with great precision and started to tie the strings of her portfolio. Guy Gerrard leant forward and stilled her hands by the simple expedient of closing his long fingers over them. Startled, she turned her head and found herself looking directly into intensely blue eyes. There was a question in their depths that she did not understand; that she did not want to understand.

'What about if he wants to make love to you?'

Robin froze. Ignoring it, Gerrard detached her suddenly nerveless hands from the strings of the portfolio and raised first one and then the other to his lips.

She said in a suffocated voice, 'I don't want . . .'

'But I do.' There was amusement in the quiet voice as he gently drew her tense body back among the cushions. 'And so will you.' A whisper of a touch along her cheekbone, her jaw, as he inexorably turned her to face him. 'You will want what I want; I promise.'

He was immensely skilful. Even as she gave herself up to his hands, Robin recognised, a little bitterly, that they were the hands of a master. His touch was gentle but very sure and, though he did nothing to alarm her, he made it plain that he would not brook resistance. Robin felt like a musical intrument, a thing beautiful enough when played upon with skill and passion, but otherwise silent and without expression.

Suddenly furious, she began to kiss him in her turn, fiercely.

That was the turning point. It was after that, as Robin subsequently realised, that Guy Gerrard stopped playing whatever private, mischievous game he had been indulging in up to then, and reached for her in earnest. So what happened next was really all her own fault.

She heard him murmur something huskily; she could not catch the words but she knew it could not be her name. He didn't know her Christian name. His mouth moved over her face, her throat, the soft skin of her shoulders that his seeking fingers had exposed and Robin moaned. She turned her head blindly, seeking his lips with her own.

She had never felt like this before. She had never even dreamed that she could feel like this. The last time she had been crushed against a man's body like this she had been desperate with fear and embarrassment, cringing with shame. She had never thought she would ever invite such intimacies.

But as Guy Gerrard stroked her clothes and her fears away between kisses, Robin recognised dimly that the old terror had gone. She was tremulous, true, a little bewildered by her body's reponse and not quite sure how to deal with it, but there was no more paralysing panic. She felt exhilarated, a little light-headed from the brandy, and full of a queer hollow longing. When he raised his head, she clung to him, her body arching involuntarily along the length of his own.

Gerrard caught his breath, looking down at her with an unfathomable expression. 'You've got the eyes of a lion,' he said softly. 'Golden and dangerous. Do you know what you're doing?'

Her head was spinning. She held his gaze for a long moment. Then she raised herself deliberately on her elbow and reached out a hand to unbutton his shirt. He caught and trapped her fingers.

'Are you certain that this is what you want?'

But Robin was not listening. She was watching the mobile mouth and feeling unmistakable desire curl up through her blood. She felt brave and reckless. She leant forward and touched his mouth with her tongue, at first tentatively then, as she felt his instinctive response, with more assurance, parting his lips.

'Robin!'

He slammed her back into the cushions and was kissing her with feverish hunger, his hands no longer gentle. Robin met his kiss eagerly, moulding his smooth back with the palms of her hands. He gave a little growl, half choked off in a laugh.

'Yes, darling. You're dynamite, aren't you?' He lifted himself, away stroking a strand of leaf-brown hair away from his mouth. 'Deceptive dynamite. You don't look all that incendiary.'

She stared at him through half-closed lids, dazed with so much unexpected feeling. The lean, enigmatic face was compellingly attractive. But she wished he did not look so serious. In fact, the expression in the blue eyes was almost bitter. She put up a hand to soothe the savage lines about his eyes, her lips parting.

Guy Gerrard gave a little movement of his shoulders; it was almost a shrug. Then he caught hold of her hand and drew it round the back of his neck. He slid one arm under her knees, the other behind her back and stood up, lifting her neatly against his chest.

'Whatever you say,' he remarked casually, as if in answer to something Robin had said, though she had not spoken. 'But not on the sitting-room sofa. I like to take my pleasures in comfort these days.'

On which practical note he strode across the room and through a hallway before entering the silent darkness of his bedroom. The door was kicked shut behind him.

CHAPTER FOUR

So now she knew that everything they said about the next morning was true, Robin thought with painful wryness. She was sitting at her desk in the mid-morning sunlight with a number of unread letters spread out before her. She should have gone to the house in Hill Place and when she walked into the mews office had been met with raised eyebrows to which she had responded by saying vaguely that she would go when she had dealt with the outstanding letters.

Then she had fled into her own room and glared so fiercely at anyone who tried to enter that her colleagues had all backed out, convinced that she really was busy.

But she had done nothing. The folders stayed unopened, the letters unanswered. And Robin had spent most of her time staring blankly into space trying, and failing, to work out what she would do next.

She shifted in her chair, wincing a little. Guy Gerrard had been anything but brutal but her body harboured a deep ache this morning. She had not noticed it last night when at last she had fallen asleep curled up in his arms. All she had been aware of then was exhaustion overlying a profound sense of peaceful well-being. In the morning, of course, it was different.

The colour stormed into her cheeks at the memory of that and all that had gone before. She dropped her head in her hands.

After he lowered her gently to the bed he moved to put on the light but Robin had stopped him. She did not want him to be able to see her face. That would place her too nakedly in his hands.

He laughed softly. 'Shy? Surely not.'

She did not answer that, at least not with words, reaching up to touch him and pull him down on the bed beside her. He did not resist.

She could not remember how he had removed her clothes or where they had gone to. All she knew was the touch of his hands, careful, sure and infinitely exciting. Her last residual fears had flown. For the first time a man's hands on her body did not recall old and bitter memories. Robin's whole consciousness was filled with nothing but this man and the exquisite sensations he was arousing.

He stroked her skin softly, her throat, her lifting breasts, her hip, the softness of her inner thigh. Robin felt as if everywhere he touched had been brought tingling to life. She did not feel intruded on, even when he sought and found places where she had never been touched before. She shivered like a pleasured animal as the clever questing fingers brought a response like molten gold surging through her veins.

Guy Gerrard was murmuring something. She would know his voice for ever now, with its characteristic undertone of laughter. He was laughing now, sounding warm and happy as his lips followed the path set out by his hands. And then, suddenly, he was laughing no longer, his voice was husky, his breathing harsh and, for a moment, his body absolutely still. Then, very slowly he raised himself on one elbow and ran his tongue along Robin's lower lip. Her whole body jerked and arched up to him in a mute plea.

It was after that, Robin thought ruefully, that he was not quite so gentle and she had no one to blame but herself. He had been trembling, tense with controlled desire. She understood that: had she not felt the same? And when he took her she had cried out, in surprise. There was somewhere a distinct pain but more than that, deeper inside her, there was a whirlwind, a flame which rose to meet him and throw them both high, high into the air to ride the tornado.

Now, in her office, she found that her hands were still trembling at the recollection.

Oh God, she thought, what have I done? What have I let him do to me? Is this what he offered Lamia that scared her so? Or—and a stab of real pain like poison in the gut at the thought—was it more than an offer? Did she make love with him, as I have done, and then find herself unable to face him in the morning?

Robin swallowed at the thought. She herself, awaking dishevelled in an unknown bed, had had a moment of pure panic. Guy was not there. His pillow had been straightened and he had, presumably, drawn the covers up over her shoulder when he left because she had the most peculiar feeling of having been tucked in.

But he was gone. And so—she perceived, struggling up on to her elbow to look round—were his clothes. She shook her head trying to clear it. Her watch had stopped; she did not know what the time was. From the light filtering through the curtains she thought it was early, maybe six o'clock. He was unlikely to have gone to work.

Robin strained, listening. She could not make out any sounds inside the flat, other than her own hard-beating heart. She slid out of bed, blushing at her nakedness and wrapped the bed cover round her. Her clothes, she discovered, had been folded neatly and placed on a satin-covered chair. She blushed again, thinking how they must have been strewn across the bedroom floor after last night's abandoned interlude.

She gathered them up. If she could find a bathroom she could just run her hands under the cold tap, scramble into her clothes and leave, now, before she had to face some arriving cleaning lady or, worse, Guy Gerrard in person. Robin found that she could not bear to think about her next encounter with Guy Gerrard. The imagined prospect of it made her wince.

So she tiptoed through the flat as if she were some storybook heroine escaping from a wizard. The bathroom was easily found. It was steamy too, which clearly indicated that he had been here in the all too-recent past. She dressed and, in the absence of a comb, ran one of his brushes over her tumbled curls.

Then she went in search of the stairway. She was certain it would be there: he had not denied it last night, after all. And it was. She even found it quite easily, at the far end of the long central corridor. She moved silently on the deep-piled carpet. She could hear him, now, in the kitchen perhaps, whistling cheerfully. He must not catch her before she could make her getaway. She slipped through the heavy door, hearing the latch close with a thunderous click behind her, and was pelting down the stone stairs as fast as her legs would take her. She did not realise that she still had her shoes in her hand until she got to the bottom.

After that it was easy. There was a heavy fire door at the bottom of the staircase, barred but unlocked. She went out into the early morning sunlight, into the square and hailed a taxi to take her home.

The telephone rang. For a moment Robin looked at it with dislike. Then, sighing faintly, she picked it up. After all there was no point in telling everyone she had to be here to work if she then refused to do just that.

It was Sally, her voice oddly formal. 'A call for you.' She put her extension down at once before Robin could ask who was calling or what they wanted. This in itself was so unusual that Robin's eyebrows flew up in astonishment. It was almost as if Sally did not want to be questioned.

She said, 'Robin Dale,' into the mouthpiece.

'Robin,' said an unknown masculine voice on the other end of the telephone, thoughtfully. 'Odd. On the Marina notepaper it gives you as Miss M. J. Dale. Where did the Robin come from?'

It was him! Robin's stomach clenched painfully. She had not recognised his voice at first because of the distorting effect of the telephone line but she did so now. Had she not heard it all last night, as he whispered practised passion against her skin? She did not think she would ever forget the hushy timbre with its constant undertone of laughter.

She swallowed hard and said coolly into the telephone, 'Good morning Mr Gerrard.'

There was a little silence.

Then he said, amused but steely, 'My name, as you very well know, is Guy. Use it.'

She whitened, glad that he could not see her. 'I don't think that would be very—professional,' she managed at last.

'*Professional?*' Guy said incredulously. 'You have to be joking.'

'N-no. I think it very important to maintain a—well, an arm's length relationship, if you like, with clients.'

Another spine-tingling pause before he said with soft menace, 'You've got a queer idea of what constitutes arm's length, Robin Dale. You were *in* my arms last night and I couldn't have got any closer if I'd melted to pure essence and poured myself inside you. How do you square that with your required client relationship?'

'I can't,' she admitted readily, her voice low. 'I——'

'Broke all your own rules did you?' he taunted her.

She felt heat wash into her cheeks again. Would she never be free from the scalding memory of her own wantonness?

'Yes,' she said in a stifled voice.

Unexpectedly he gave a rueful laugh. 'Well, if it's any comfort, so did I. The cold light of day was something of a shock this morning.'

Robin felt as if she had been stabbed to the heart. So he had awoken to faint surprise at his own behaviour. And regret too, it was plain from his reflective voice. She could not reasonably expect anything else, she told herself. Nevertheless to hear it in those meditative tones hurt almost unbearably.

'I believe you,' she said, struggling to sound friendly and sympathetic but basically indifferent. She ended up, even to her own ears, sounding wooden.

'And finding you gone did not help. I could have sworn you were asleep when I got up,' he finished interrogatively.

The odd, wrong, intimacy of the question was like pressure on an unhealed wound. Robin could hardly bring herself to answer. 'I—don't remember.'

'No?' Guy sounded puzzled. 'Do you remember why you went pelting off down the fire escape without a word, as if I were some sort of Bluebeard?'

'I was busy. I had to get to work.'

'At six o'clock in the morning?' Guy mocked gently.

'I—I had things to do at home that I meant to do last night,' Robin said desperately. That was better, she thought, that sounded plausible, even probable. 'I thought you were probably working, too. I didn't want to disturb you.' And that sounded positively true.

He said evenly, 'You lie through your teeth. As you must have known if you'd come looking for me, even if it was only to say goodbye. But you didn't did you, Robin Dale? You made damned sure you kept out of my way and you took off like a rocket the moment the coast was clear. I want to know why.'

There was that steel again, the inflexible purpose of a man used to imposing his will on others.

Robin said weakly, 'Does it matter?'

'Yes,' came the uncompromising answer at once.

'What if my reasons were private?'

'You surrendered your privacy last night.' His voice warmed into laughter again. 'Pretty drastically, as I recall.'

Robin jumped as if she had been stung, as much at that laughing, intimate tone as at what he said, though that, too, horrified her.

'I surrendered nothing last night,' she told him violently. 'Do you understand that? Nothing.'

Guy Gerrard said softly, 'But we both know that's not true, don't we, Robin?'

She shrank away from the telephone as if it was alive and had spat poison at her.

'What do you mean?' she whispered fearfully.

'I mean,' he said deliberately, 'that I hadn't expected a sophisticated lady to be as untouched as you were.'

She drew a ragged breath which must have been audible to him. So he had known.

His voice gentled. 'That was another of my nightmares, this morning. I don't often suffer from guilt but I wasn't too keen on myself at breakfast. Especially as you'd run from me as if you expected to be raped.'

'No,' she managed in a strangled whisper.

'Look, I don't think it's very profitable discussing this on the telephone. When can I see you?'

'You can't.' Her reply was instinctive and unequivocal, fuelled by panic. 'I'm busy.'

'I know that,' Guy said impatiently. 'So am I, for God's sake. I fly out of the country this evening. But even I rearrange my schedule for important things.'

Robin said in a voice she did not recognise, 'This—is—not—important.'

'Don't be silly.' He brushed it aside. 'When are you coming down to Hill Place? I went there this morning but the workmen told me you hadn't put in an appearance and I had to go off to a meeting. But I could meet you there now. Or anywhere else you care to name.'

'No!' she said forcefully.

'Look, Robin,' he was patient, 'you must see we've got things to discuss. I was working on totally false assumptions last night. And they weren't all my fault. God knows, I'm not proud of myself but you went out of your way to present yourself as a woman of the world who had seen it all.'

'Oh quite.' Robin was brittle but composed. 'Please don't think I'm blaming you for anything. You don't have to apologise.'

'Apologies were not exactly what I had in mind,' Guy said drily. 'A bit of straight talking was what I was after.'

Robin said, 'I don't think that would be very useful.'

'Maybe you don't. I think it's essential. Now where do we meet?'

'We don't,' she told him coolly. 'Not today and not, *probably* not, ever again. You may want to talk to me but I'm afraid I don't want to see you.'

'Robin,' he interrupted, 'are you *afraid* of me?'

That was far too close to the truth to be comfortable. 'Of course not,' she snapped.

'Then why . . .?'

'I made a mistake last night,' she said flatly. 'I'm not proud of myself either, if you must know. But I don't want to go turning over the pieces. I've done it. I wish I hadn't. I have to live with that. And I want to put the whole thing out of my mind as soon as possible.'

There was a pause, even longer than before.

'I see,' he said at last, softly. 'So that's it.'

'The work on your house will be completed on time, I give you my word,' she said briskly. 'I shall see to it myself, though I don't promise to be on the premises all the time.' She allowed herself a wintry laugh. 'You are rather getting through our lady designers at the speed of light, aren't you? But I promise that the contract will be fulfilled by the date we agreed.'

'What do you mean?' he interjected swiftly.

'Just to do my job,' Robin assured him.

'No, not that. About me getting through your lady designers.'

She gave an angry laugh, suddenly recalling in bitterness Lamia's scared little face and trembling voice. At last the distress fell away from her in a blast of pure, revivifying fury.

'Oh, you'll probably have forgotten,' she said sweetly. 'Lamia Frizell was the one you terrified out of her wits *last* week.'

'What the blazes are you talking about?' Guy sounded really angry now, the laughter quite banished.

'I'm talking about how you seem to be unable to keep your hands off your employees,' she said nastily. It was unfair, at least in her own case, she knew; she had invited him as plainly as possible to take exactly what he had taken. But she was angry, with ten years' worth of stored anger against the male sex, and it was not only on her own behalf. 'And though I am, of course, flattered that you wish to continue the pursuit, in my own case I can state categorically that once is enough. I am sorry,' she ended insincerely, 'if that wounds your self-esteem but it is the truth. Please keep away from me in future.'

She put the telephone down with a force that helped to relieve her feelings. Then, almost immediately, she picked it up again and buzzed Sally.

'If Mr Gerrard calls again for me, you are to say that I am out,' she instructed her. Her voice was still shaking with fury. 'Not unavailable. Out. And you don't know when I'll be back. He can leave any messages he wants with you but he is *not* to come here.'

Sally was silent momentarily, clearly stunned.

'But Robin, I can't stop him. He knows the address. If he wants to come here for any reason, he will,' she protested faintly.

'If he turns up, I want to know before anyone else does. And I won't see him,' said Robin between her teeth.

'You've had a row with him,' Sally diagnosed.

'You could put it like that.' Robin's natural sense of humour reasserted itself suddenly. She chuckled, thinking of Sally's protectiveness of the agency. 'At least, if you don't want the eyes of Marina's most influential client clawed out with enthusiasm, you will keep him out of my range. OK?'

For the rest of the day Robin worked like a demon. She went briefly to the house in Hill Place where a friendly plumber told her that Mr Gerrard had been, and looked as if he was in a terrible temper when he did not find her there. There was a good deal of sympathy in his account. Miss Dale was a nice, sensible lady and a good prompt payer. She deserved more consideration. He had heard Mr Gerrard swearing when Bill had told him Miss Dale had not come down from the office and they had both been shocked by his language.

''Ad a bit of a night on the tiles, I shouldn't wonder,' he told Robin consolingly. 'Looked like 'ell, 'e did, this morning.'

Robin thanked him hollowly for his information.

Fortunately there were no problems at the house and she was able to leave. She did not go to the office but went straight to the workshop of an upholsterer who often did work for Marina Interiors. He was making chairs for Guy Gerrard's new drawing room and had asked her to go and check on the colour of the velvet which had arrived. She chose the one she wanted, a deep gun metal grey, the colour of storm clouds. Geoff looked dubious.

'Won't it be a bit dull like?' he asked.

Robin smiled. 'Not with the rest of the room. And lots of lemon and apricot cushions as well. Look.' And she showed him her watercolour drawing of the finished room as she imagined it.

'That's pretty,' he said at last approvingly. 'And I like them curtains.'

They were a woodland chintz in tones of walnut and amber. Robin had designed it herself when she had been unable to find a print she felt happy with for the drawing room. It was in the process of being printed.

'Hand blocked,' she told him. 'I did the block.'

He was impressed and said so. She was pleased, turning to the leaf which had the design in detail painted on it.

'There you are. That's it.' She considered it herself, her head on one side, pondering. 'I was wondering about having one of the Victorian chairs covered in it, to be honest, instead of the wickerwork pattern.' She nodded across the room to one of the bales of his stock. 'It would be a lot more expensive of course, but it would still be well within the budget I've been given.' She looked at the hessian-covered Victorian chair in the corner of the workroom, measuringly. 'What do you think, Geoff?'

'I wouldn't spoil the ship for a ha'porth of tar. But you know the client. Would he kick up a fuss about the expense? Is he the type?'

Robin gave a little choke of laughter. 'I think he's the type to kick up a fuss about anything he chooses. But, no, he hasn't been difficult about money. So far,' she added as another thought struck her. She grimaced, not liking the tenor of her thoughts. 'No, what I really meant, Geoff, was do you think it too feminine? It's a man's drawing room after all.'

'*I* like it,' he told her. 'I don't think it's feminine at all, not that leaf and hedgerow design. But then I like chintz. Some people think prints of whatever kind are— well, you know—a bit soft. But if he's approved the curtains he can't be one of those.'

'No,' she agreed thoughtfully.

She had not discussed the designs with him. Marina had done that. He was an old friend of hers apparently, or a friend of a friend. The contract had been concluded after lengthy negotiations that spanned a number of social evenings. Recalling that Robin wondered, suddenly and sharply, whether Marina, too, was one of his conquests. Her mouth went dry.

'Who's the chap?' asked Geoff, screwing his head round to read the name of the assignment in the bottom right-hand corner of the designs in Robin's neat printing. 'Hill Place, eh? *Very* up-market. Good lord, *him*,' he added in a changed tone, almost one of awe. 'I didn't know you worked for Guy Gerrard.'

'We haven't done before.' Robin sighed faintly. 'And I'm very much afraid we won't again.' She gave him a long look. 'And that's not for repeating, Geoff.'

'Cross my heart and hope to die,' he assured her solemnly. He gave a soft whistle. 'But you're flying high, now, aren't you? I saw a piece on him in the paper the other day that said his family was one of the ten richest in the world. And he runs the lot since his dad died. Good few years ago, that was.'

'It shows,' Robin said ruefully. 'He's not used to not getting his own way.'

Geoff cocked an eyebrow at her. 'Don't like him, do you?'

She shrugged. 'Not a lot. But then, I don't have to.'

'He's not had an easy time of it, by all accounts,'

Geoff said, watching her. 'There's money in the family, of course, but his dad was bankrupt when he died. The mother had a nervous breakdown and he was left holding the baby. Literally they say, because his sister was only a child; and the mother obviously couldn't look after her. Can't have been much fun taking care of her with his money worries and all. Especially as she turned out a right young tearaway.'

'Where did you find all this out, Geoff?' Robin asked, intrigued. 'I hadn't figured you for a gossip column reader.'

The upholsterer gave her a grin. 'I'm not. But my mum and my Alice are. No, there was an article on the tycoons in one of the colour supplements a month or so back and I remember him from that. He was the youngest by a fair few years and my Alice said she thought he was the only one of them as was fanciable, money or no money. Seemed a good-looking chap, by his photograph.'

Robin swallowed. She recalled the lean, rangy body, the chiselled jaw line, watchful eyes full of mockery, the hard mouth with its hint of sensuality that could soften into devastating gentleness against a woman's skin.

'Yes,' she said. 'He's attractive all right.'

'And you still don't like him?' He sounded incredulous. 'Not with *his* looks and money?'

She stood up. 'One of the few things I've learned in my life, Geoff, and I learnt it early, is that attractive men are seldom likeable. Nor are the rich, quite often. They don't have to try, you see. The rest of us need other people's co-operation, so we're helpful and supportive to our fellow men. People like Guy Gerrard and his kind can get everything they want without having to do that.'

He said soberly, 'That's a bad way to think, Robin.

There's a lot of bitterness once you set out on that road.'

Her smile was a little twisted. 'I'm not setting out. It's a road I've been on for ten years.'

Geoff shook his head as if he could not credit his ears. 'I'd never have thought it of you.'

'You're not the only one who doesn't approve,' Robin said ruefully, thinking of Sally Jackson. 'I've been picking up a lot of flack in the last two days. But I can't help the way I am.'

She repacked her portfolio and zipped it closed, placing it carefully under her arm. He came with her to her car, his face disturbed, the kindly eyes anxious.

'You ought to talk to someone about that chip you've got on your shoulder,' he told her frankly. 'If it were me, I'd not have got away with it for ten years; my mum would have knocked it out of me. What does your mum say?'

There was a certain irony there, Robin acknowledged to herself, though Geoff would not appreciate it. She slid into her treasured sports car and he closed the door for her courteously. She looked up at him, before starting the engine.

'I expect my mother would agree with you,' she said coolly. 'She was a great one for letting bygones be bygones and turning the other cheek. I can't say that it ever did her much good but I suppose she enjoyed it. I haven't seen her for years.'

Geoff looked down at her, even more worried. 'Your dad?'

'My father died when I was a child. And no, Geoff, before you ask, I'm missing grandparents, brothers and sisters and fairy godmothers as well.' Her voice was light, teasing. 'An orphan of the storm in fact.'

'There must be someone. Marina, maybe? No,' he agreed with her silent mocking incredulity. Marina was gifted, glamorous and highly articulate, but she was not the sort of person to be readily confided in. 'No, not Marina. Well,' he shuffled his feet a little in embarrassment, 'you know you're always welcome to come and see Alice and me any time. Any time at all,' he said with emphasis.

Robin was touched. 'You're very kind, Geoff. I'll remember that.' She started the car. 'But I'm not in any trouble, you know. I may have got a client I don't like very much but it doesn't constitute a major crisis in my life. There aren't any rapids ahead.'

Geoff sniffed. 'I shouldn't be too sure of that,' he said. 'I've seen his photograph.'

But Robin laughed, tossing her hair back from her face, and let in the clutch. Geoff stepped back, raising his hand in a salute, and the powerful car shot away.

CHAPTER FIVE

ROBIN drove back slowly to the office with none of her accustomed dash. She had, she thought, been very rash in asserting that there were no rapids ahead. She hoped she would see no more of Guy Gerrard but she was by no means sure that he would accept dismissal so easily. After all, she had more or less hung up on him and she did not think he was used to that.

She eased the car into its parking place at the end of the mews. Switching off the engine she sat thoughtfully for a moment without opening the door. It was very warm and quiet, the shriek of the West End traffic little more than a murmur from the distance. For a timeless moment she did not move, thinking.

Guy knew that she had been a virgin. He had made that very clear on the telephone. Well, she would rather he had not known but there was nothing she could do about it now. Except make sure that that did not put her in his power.

Robin thought wryly how she had threatened him that she fought fire with fire. There was vainglory for you. She had had no idea, until he took her in his arms, what passion could be like. She had no way of fighting what she felt; but that did not mean that she had no way of fighting him.

In the enclosed silence of the car she gave a little sigh, almost of regret. There had been times last night when she had felt as if they had known each other for years. For a moment it had almost felt as if he came to her, overburdened by those responsibilities he had spoken of, for love and comfort. Robin gave herself a mental shake. There was no question of love: that had to be nonsense. Quite apart from his reputation, there was the new lady that Lamia had spoken of in his life. And there was the way he had behaved to Lamia herself. Yes, that was the way to resist him; concentrate on the harm he had done Lamia.

The trouble was, she thought wryly, that thinking of Guy with Lamia caused more than a twinge of jealousy to assail Robin herself. But that had to be nonsense. She did not know him; what she knew of him she disliked. He was the type of man she had learned early to fear and to avoid. And even if he was not quite that type—well, what was it that Sally had said? That Robin was afraid of getting involved? That had given her a nasty shock; it was altogether too close to the truth. Not because she had ever got too close to anybody herself but because her mother had done precisely that and Robin had seen how it had warped and contaminated her until she saw nothing straight. Her mother's view had been distorted permanently by what Francis had told her, so that in the end she had no forbearance, not even when it came to hurting her own daughter.

Robin did not blame her mother. It was easy to see how it happened. And, though she had been almost desperate with disillusion and despair at the time, mature hindsight helped. When her mother had poured out her woes to the newshounds she had probably been in no better state than her daughter. No, Robin did not blame her mother. But she blamed her stepfather, profoundly, and she promised herself that no man—no man, no matter who he was or how charming he seemed—was going to have that influence on herself.

So Sally was right. To the extent that Robin meant to keep her vision clear and uninfluenced by a man, she meant also to make sure that she did not get deeply involved.

So where did that leave her with Guy Gerrard? There was no doubt that he had got closer to her than any other man had ever managed. Robin's mouth curled wryly. He had got closer than any of her friends would have believed possible. She almost did not believe it herself. And the disturbing thing was that she did not know why.

He was everything that she was most suspicious of in a man. And no matter how extraordinary last night's events might seem to her, it was plain that for Guy there was nothing very out of the way in meeting a woman for the first time, finding himself attracted to her and so taking her to bed. Robin shivered suddenly, violently. No, she could not handle that. It was foreign to her nature, her tastes, her deepest principles. She must keep away from him at all costs. And put him out of her mind.

Resolved, she jumped out of the car and hurried into the office.

'Hi,' said Sally, looking up. 'You're in demand.'

Robin tensed. 'Phone messages?' Had Guy rung back, in spite of her words?

Sally nodded to the memory board. 'Marina. Your godfather twice.'

'Felix?' Robin was instantly anxious. 'Is something wrong? How did he sound? Ill? Worried?'

Sally grinned. Felix Lament was a gentleman of the old school.

'He chatted me up pretty comprehensively on both occasions,' she said frankly.

'Ah.' Robin relaxed. 'Felix on his normal form. That's a relief. I suppose I'd better find out what he wants, though. I'll ring Marina after that.'

And Sally, though she had the highest sense of responsibility to one's employers, had no fault to find with Robin's priorities.

Felix, in spite of the uncharacteristic urgency of his second message, sounded unruffled when she telephoned him. Would Robin be a dear girl and come round to see him tonight? No, it was nothing serious, just a few people in for drinks now that he was back; all very spur of the moment, or he would have sent her a proper invitation. He heard she was becoming very successful; he felt like basking in her reflected glory.

Robin laughed as she put the telephone down. Felix was much too famous in his own right for her to take his last remark as anything but gentle teasing. Anyway, he did not care about fame. And as for success—well, Robin had achieved that with her directorship of Marina Interiors; and when she won the Casa de Flores prize. There had been no outstanding achievement, no milestone, recently.

Unless he had somehow heard about the Gerrard contract? Robin's eyebrows twitched together in a disturbed frown. Felix was an inveterate gossip—even though he had been the soul of discretion on the subject of what had driven her from her mother's home and her own burgeoning career ten years ago—and it was perfectly possible that he had picked up that little item of news. The circumstances in which he might have picked it up, made her blood run cold. Felix knew a lot of influential people—it was only the rich who could afford to buy his paintings, after all—and it was more than likely that Guy Gerrard was one.

But then Robin gave herself a shake. She was becoming paranoid. It was ridiculous. Gerrard knew where to contact her, how to find her. If he had made no direct move to do so during the day, and it was clear that he had not, there was no reason why he should go to work indirectly on her friends. Quite apart from the fact that it was needlessly complicated, Robin judged that it would be out of character for him.

No, he had probably flown out already, shrugging off last night's encounter. She had made it plain that she did not want to see him again. And she did not flatter herself that she was so devastatingly attractive that a man like Gerrard would pursue her once she made it clear that she was not interested. There were too many others, all more beautiful, more charming, more *fun*, who were available.

She got up and went to the gilt mirror above the fireplace, looking at herself seriously. Perversely, she found she was more than a little envious of her imagined successful rivals. Except, of course, that they were not rivals because she, Robin Dale, did not want Guy Gerrard.

'I do not want him,' she said out loud to the face in the mirror and then gave a little surprised laugh at her own intensity.

It was a pleasant enough face, she judged, without being special: the features were regular, the bones elegant. Only the long-lashed amber eyes were in any way special, though with those heavy eyebrows, they could make her look very fierce sometimes. She remembered that Guy Gerrard had said she had the eyes of a lion and bit her lip. She had certainly been fierce with him, several times. It was not surprising if he did not want to see her again.

Perhaps he had even withdrawn the contract? Perhaps he had been in touch with Marina in Tuscany and told her that her fellow director was not giving satisfaction. Robin could hardly blame him in the circumstances. She squared her shoulders. Sally had said that Marina wanted to talk to her and there was no sense in putting it off.

She went back to the desk, buzzed Sally and asked her to get the Italian number that Marina had left.

'Hello, darling? Hello? *Hello?*' As always on the

telephone, Marina sounded imperious and faintly frantic. 'Robin, are you there?'

'Yes,' said Robin composedly.

'I hate foreign phones,' said Marina unncessarily. 'They confuse me. I've got a list of what I want to say somewhere. Wait.'

Robin did as she was told while, from Marina's end of the line, there came the sound of tumbling objects and muted cursing.

'Bloody magazines,' said Marina in parenthesis. 'I've just knocked over a century of *House and Garden*. Now *where. . .?*'

Again, from behind her, Robin could hear the muted tones of an unmistakably masculine voice. Her smile was wry. Of course. Marina might announce that she was exhausted and had to get away absolutely on her own for a while but, being Marina, that phrase was bound to encompass a man's presence. Robin had never known her temperamental managing director to last for more than a couple of weeks without the sexual companionship of some devoted man. And it would be utterly unrealistic to expect that she would go on holiday alone.

It was one of the major differences between them. When they were in disagreement, Marina would fling it at Robin that she was a cold fish who could not design houses for real warm-blooded people. Marina tended to work too hard and let off steam in enjoyable Central European rages during which she was diabolically insulting and after which, contrite, she was wildly generous. The personnel of Marina Interiors were philosophical equally about her tantrums and her oppressive remorse afterwards.

Marina might be working herself up to a temper now. The voice behind her was clearly placatory.

'But I *told* you when he rang to write it down at once

on that thing on the wall . . .' she could be heard saying in a rising tone.

Robin contemplated asking her whether she was having a good holiday, decided against it, and waited patiently.

'Are you still there, darling?' Marina sounded marginally less frantic. 'I've found my list. Now . . .' and she launched into a parade of trivial reminders, every one of which Sally had already recorded or dealt with.

Robin wrote them down dutifully, a frown gathering. She could see no reason for this. It might be of course that Marina, who had not been away from the business for longer than a couple of days for several years now, felt insecure without her finger on the pulse and needed to reassure herself that the office had not burned down in her absence. But, on the other hand, even when she was present, Marina was not a great one for minutiae. Detail bored Marina and she made no secret of the fact. These were the sort of matters that normally she would have left to Sally Jackson, anyway.

When she had finished, Robin said carefully, 'Are you sure that's all, Marina? You didn't want anything else?'

'Just to hear a nice English voice, darling,' Marina said airily. 'Speaking Italian is such an *effort*; so operatic, even to buy a pound of butter.' She paused and then added, 'Unless you've got anything to tell me? Any delicious gossip?'

'Nothing,' said Robin a trifle grimly. So Marina was fishing after all.

'How is my darling Guy's house?'

'All right.'

'Has he told you that that hellcat of a sister of his is coming back to live with him?' Marina asked. 'I suppose it's the only way to keep her out of reform school but I pity him. He'll have to become *frightfully* respectable, which won't suit him at all.'

Robin said, 'I hadn't heard, no. But he has made one or two changes to the house design. I suppose he must be giving her the balcony room on the third floor as a sort of bedsit: he's told me to put fitted cupboards and bookshelves in there and a small vanitory unit.'

'Ah,' said Marina knowingly. 'That would be it. He didn't tell you?'

'We didn't,' said Robin misleadingly though sticking to the letter of the truth, 'talk about personal things.'

'No, I suppose he wouldn't.' Marina sighed. 'It's very hard on him. Did you know the girl ran away with some tennis pro and they thought she'd been kidnapped? Apparently she sent Guy's stepmother a ransom note, the little monkey.' Marina's voice was full of a reluctant admiration. 'It's all over the Italian press. Of course Laurel is pretty as a picture and they are a bit—well—sensitive about *kidnapping* over here. I believe poor old Rose had to come over here and collect her from police custody. Guy must be *furious*.'

'He sounds as if he would have every reason to be,' observed Robin.

'Has he been in a terrible passion with you, darling? He does tend to lay about him on all sides when things don't go his way.'

So he had telephoned Marina. There could be no other explanation for this sudden interest. Though it was difficult to account for the solicitude. Robin would have expected Marina to be spitting like a Roman candle if she thought her assistant had been offending a favoured—not to say beloved—client.

She said bluntly, 'Has Mr Gerrard been complaining to you, Marina?'

'Darling, no.' She sounded really startled. 'What an

extraordinary idea. He was very complimentary, let me tell you.'

'You've spoken to him?'

'Yes. Well, I had to telephone Rose to find out about Laurel—and say how sorry I was, of course,—and Guy happened to be there. He'd just brought them back from the airport.'

'When was this?'

Robin held her breath for Marina's answer.

'Oh, lunchtime-ish,' she said vaguely.

'Today?'

'Well, of course today. The story didn't really break until this morning's papers. Why?'

'Did he really not say anything about me?' asked Robin tensely.

Marina gave a little laugh. 'You've been fighting with him,' she deduced, in apparent delight. 'I thought you would if you ever got to meet him. And so I told him.'

'What? What did he say about me?'

'Oh, he was perfectly polite,' Marina assured her. 'Full of praise for the work you'd put in and how you'd helped him with the changes to the design.'

'But?' prompted Robin, hearing the reservation.

'Well, he was a *little* unforthcoming when I asked him how you'd got on.'

Robin closed her eyes: how they'd got on, dear God!

'Was he?' she asked faintly.

'So I told him not to be surprised if you didn't fall at his feet the way most stupid women do. I said to him, "She's a simple working girl with a heart of stone and she doesn't like men like you, who are *too* attractive for the world's good." And you don't, do you, darling?'

'What did he say to that?' Robin felt a great hollow open at her feet. She refused to contemplate it.

'Very chilly,' Marina told her in amusement. 'Shut me up at once. Not another word on the subject. If you

ask me,' she said reflectively, 'you've annoyed him. It would be beneath his dignity to admit it, of course. But it must be years since he met a woman who didn't start drivelling the moment he smiled at her. I assume, you didn't by the way, darling?'

'Didn't drivel?' echoed Robin, smiling bitterly. 'Oh no, Marina, I didn't drivel. And I can safely promise you that I won't.'

'Good. That takes a weight off my mind. Because I did *rather* get the impression that gorgeous Guy might have designs on you. From something he said.'

'What?' demanded Robin, sitting bolt upright.

'Oh, it may have been nothing. But it was when I told him that you weren't keen on any men, particularly the tall, dark and handsome division: he said that was a pity.' She paused, probably for effect. 'And that somebody ought to do something about it. Oh, I'm being called away; the baker seems to have arrived. See you soon, darling. Love to everyone.' She gave a little laugh and added with what Robin thought was quite unnecessary emphasis, 'Be good.'

She rang off. For a moment Robin sat as if turned to stone, the dead telephone buzzing in her hand. Then, very slowly, she replaced it.

What was the man up to? Had he really made that worrying remark or was Marina simply embroidering the truth for her own amusement? Robin knew that she was perfectly capable of it.

She tried to tell herself that it was all a storm in a teacup; that she would not see him again. He was, after all, a very busy man with a lot of commitments elsewhere. Besides, by what Marina was saying, he had his hands more than full with his family problems at the moment. There was small chance that he would have the time or the interest to pursue her reluctant self any further.

Robin gave a little sigh, stretching herself back in her chair. It was only when she tautened and then deliberately relaxed the muscles in the back of her neck that she realised how tense she had been.

She gave a wry smile. Marina would say that that was what came of staying a virgin until you were twenty-eight, if Marina ever found out, the very thought of which made Robin's blood run cold. And certainly there had been no sign of it in that cheerful conversation, thank God.

Robin stood up. Perhaps it would all blow over. She would not see Guy Gerrard again, she would get over her uncharacteristic behaviour and in time she would forget the whole thing.

She was doing a very fair job of forgetting when she arrived at Felix's flat later. A rapidly arranged visit to the hairdresser and a long scented bath had completed the process of relaxation. She was looking good too, in a cocktail dress of her favourite amber, cinched in at the waist with a gold chain. She did not normally wear much make-up but Felix liked it and so, to please him, she had brushed dramatic grey and lilac shadows on to her eyelids, with a wasp sting of lemony glitter just above the lashes.

Felix greeted this vision with delight. 'Robin, my angel, you look wonderful. Like Cleopatra in a *good* mood. What have you been doing since I last saw you to wreak this transformation?'

'Painting my face,' said Robin with a chuckle. She kissed his cheek. 'It's good to see you, Felix. How are you?'

She looked at him searchingly. His lined face was tanned but his eyes were tired. He gave a swift shrug, dismissing her concern. 'Painting everybody else's face and thriving on it. One day soon I must do yours, I think. You are getting to be a very exciting woman, little one.'

Robin was used to extravagant compliments from Felix, partly because they were part of his style, mostly because he loved her; but at this she was startled.

'*Exciting?*' she echoed disbelievingly. 'Oh really, Felix.'

'So I hear.' His elderly monkey's face looked smug. 'So they have been telling me.'

Robin's brows contracted. 'They? Who?' she asked.

But she need not have troubled. The answer was there in front of her: an answer that stood well over six feet and whose blue eyes met her own with laughing challenge in their depths.

'I believe you know each other,' said Felix unneccesarily.

Guy smiled. Robin felt her stomach contract into a knot of pure longing. She pushed it away from her consciousness. It was lust, she thought fiercely, nothing but lust.

Felix, looking pleased and rather amused, drifted tactfully away.

Robin said as coolly as she could manage, 'I thought you were on a plane out?'

The smile widened, deepening the creases on either side of the aquiline nose. It was a hawkish face, she now realised. One was so mesmerised by those startling eyes that one did not at first notice the strength of the bone structure, the arrogance with which the head was held. Oh, he might be as charming as he pleased but the charm was a thin veneer over solid steel.

The charm was much in evidence now. 'I should be,' Guy said ruefully. His eyes twinkled. 'As you know, something came up.'

His sister, of course. Robin looked round the party thoughtfully. Was she here with him?

She said sincerely, 'I'm sorry.'

The elegant brows twitched together at that. 'Yes, so I'd gathered.'

Robin stared at him, uncomprehending. Had he been talking to Marina again? To Sally Jackson?

A little impatiently, he continued, 'Look, can I get you a drink or something? Or shall we leave now?'

'Leave?'

'Yes. I'm taking you to dinner.'

Robin felt herself go pale. 'No,' she said at once, flatly. 'No. Not again.'

'You don't dine with the same man two nights in a row?' he asked dulcetly.

She prayed she was not blushing. 'I don't do anything with the same man two nights in a row,' she said coolly, meeting the wicked laughter in his eyes head on.

'I am aware.' He shifted, half turning, so that suddenly she was in a corner, talking only to him, with no possibility of being interrupted by a passing acquaintance. 'You haven't given yourself much opportunity up to now, have you? I know. I've been making enquiries.'

'You've been *what*?' Robin was outraged. 'How dare you?'

He made a little grimace. 'I tend to share your distaste. But you wouldn't talk to me, so——' an expressive shrug, a sidelong look that considered her assessingly '——I had to seek the information I needed elsewhere.'

'I do not see,' said Robin, stiff with fury, 'that you *needed* any information whatsoever beyond the fact that I did not want to see you again.'

'Then you have very little imagination,' he informed her. He paused. 'Put yourself in my place. A lady of whom you know nothing but have heard a good deal about explodes into your life and when you actually sit up and collect your wits you find she was not the product as advertised at all but something quite other. Wouldn't you feel concerned?'

'You have no need to feel concerned about me,' she said haughtily 'I am not concerned about you.'

It was an ungracious little speech and she saw him register the fact. For a moment the blue eyes iced over and she had a glimpse of what he would be like in business or combat: unmoved, ruthless. She suppressed a shudder, lifting her chin. She was not afraid of him and she would not let her treacherous body tell her that she was.

'No, you've made that very clear.' The soft voice was rueful but there was something else in it too, something allied to the steel and the ruthlessness she sensed in him. 'Then let us say that I was puzzled, if you prefer that to concern.'

'Puzzled about me?'

'Very. Understandable, wouldn't you agree?'

'And because of some idle curiosity on your part, you've been—what was it you said?—making enquiries?'

Guy nodded. His eyes were bleak. 'I have quite a full dossier. Do you want to see it?'

Panic, real unconcealable panic, shot through Robin. The amber eyes widened and she lost colour. What did he know? What had he found out? Was it going to come back to haunt her after all these years? Oh God, just one night of madness and she was back on the edge of the precipice again, with no self-respect left and precious few defences. And if he told . . .

He stared at her. 'What have I said to make you look like that?'

She took hold of herself with an effort. Her lips felt stiff, anaesthetised, and her tongue tied itself in knots. She had to take a steadying breath but in the end she managed to answer him.

'Distaste, Mr Gerrard, as you said yourself. I am surprised you felt you had to go to such lengths for a mere puzzle.' Her voice was very soft but it cut like a whip. 'Or don't you like puzzles?'

The scorn made no apparent impression on him. 'Oh, I like them.' He let his eyes wonder from her mouth to the exposed place at the base of her throat where the pulse beat frantically; then down to the taut breasts, moulded softly by the fall of amber silk.

Robin gasped, as much at his insolence as at the crazy feelings that were rioting through her. His gaze was a deliberate, intrusive thing. She felt as if he had touched her with his hands, instead of laughing eyes. More, she felt as if he had disposed of the golden material and exposed her to the eyes of everyone else in the room. She burned with resentment and a queer, breathless, shyness.

His eyes came back to hold hers, very steadily. He was wry, amused and, she thought, quite implacable.

'I adore puzzles. I always have. But not to leave them unsolved.'

She said in a hoarse voice, 'What are you going to do?'

Guy hesitated. A faint disquiet came into his face. 'What are you so afraid of?' he said at last. And when she did not answer added in a gentler tone, 'Surely not of me? You're not a child, whatever else you——' he paused and then finished steadily '—may have been.'

Robin felt her colour wash up under her skin as if she had been doused with cold water. Guy sighed, watching her. 'You must know that I——'

But she interrupted him, her voice harsh, 'I know nothing about you, Mr Gerrard. Nothing. As I said, I am not concerned about you.'

There was an incredulous silence. Then the azure eyes flickered and went blank. Robin had a horrid feeling that he had pulled down a shutter, that he was looking at her from a long way behind the startling eyes, that he was studying her in the depths of his brain to which she had no access.

'Ah,' he said at length. 'I see. You mean I have to go back to my researches from secondary sources.'

She stared at him appalled. The party was speeding up; the talk was noticeably louder than when she had arrived and in the background someone had put on a record of Felix's favourite blues. There was a tinkle of glasses, a good deal of laughter.

But the party might just as well have been happening next door or across the street for all that it impinged on them. Robin felt as if she were trapped, locked in a bubble of ice so that she could see all the warm, human friendly things going on outside but she could not break out of her prison to join them. She had never felt so cold in her life.

Guy Gerrard gave her his charming, lop-sided smile. It was not reaching his eyes any more. 'Let me put it to you this way. As I see it, you have two options. Either you come with me now and let me find out what I want to know. Or——'

Robin was dumb.

He went on hardly, 'Or I do what you're so obviously afraid of and commission a full-scale investigation.'

She closed her eyes briefly, as if at a blow.

'Because it would tell me, wouldn't it? It would tell me every damned thing I want to know.'

Even now she had to try, though she felt that her courage and common sense had all been beaten out of her in the last hours. She stretched her lips in a travesty of a smile.

'That depends on what you want to know, Mr Gerrard.'

The blue eyes flashed momentarily and were veiled at once. So there was feeling there, in that analytical inspection, though Robin did not think the feeling was very friendly.

'Oh, I imagine you're pretty clear about that,' he said coolly. 'But I'll spell it out, if you'd rather. I want to know why you threw yourself at my head last night. I want to know why, having done so, you've been running like an Olympic rabbit ever since. I want to know why you were a frightened virgin at twenty-eight.' He paused. 'Twenty-eight and four months,' he corrected himself.

He really does know everything, Robin thought, chilled as he had meant her to be.

'I want to know why you are passion itself to make love to and yet socially as icy a lady as ever I've been frozen off by. I want to know why your friends love and admire you but no man gets near—or has got near in five years. In particular, I want to know why everyone keeps telling me that you won't have anything to do with a man like me. What do you know about men like me?' He drew a long breath, laughing softly. 'So that's what I want to know, mysterious Robin Dale. For a start. And you're going to tell me. Aren't you?'

She looked round her feverishly. There was no escape route. Felix was at the far end of his colonnaded sitting room pouring wine and laughing. Nobody was so much as looking in their direction. Suddenly, looking at Felix's smiling face across the room, a horrid thought struck her. 'Have you been interrogating my godfather?'

'Interrogating?' He mused over the word. 'No, I don't think that's how I'd describe it. We talked about you. Of course. That was why he asked me here this evening, though I admit it was at my prompting.'

'Did you tell him about last night?' Robin asked quietly.

He shot her a quick look. 'Would it disturb you if I had done?'

She did not answer, biting her lip.

'How very interesting.' His voice was a drawl. 'You don't give a damn about me, though I am a valued and influential client, but you mind what Felix Lamont thinks about you. Now is that because he's a gossip or because you care for the man's good opinion?'

Oh, he was clever, thought Robin bitterly. He might just as well have a scalpel to wield he cut so cleverly to the bone. She was silent.

'An old friend,' he murmured. 'That's what they said and that's what he told me himself. I can see how old—but how friendly?'

There was a bite to the words that made Robin wince. It was not the first time that her relationship with Felix had been looked at askance. There had been raised eyebrows when he had first sponsored her designs in the showrooms of London and Paris. For a while there had been plenty of people only too happy to speculate that Felix had found himself a mistress young enough to be his daughter. It had not worried her. At the time, all that concerned her was that whatever the papers said it should not be the truth.

For over a year she had lived in dread of the reporters, the gossip columnists. Whenever the telephone rang she would freeze. She had to nerve herself every morning to take the letters out of her letter box and turn them over in case one was addressed not to Miss M. J. Dale but to Miranda Tyrell-Brown.

No, she had not minded that they thought she was Felix's lover. As long as they labelled her in that way they were unlikely to dig deeper and discover the real, unbearable, secret of her existence. But she minded now, as much for Felix as herself.

She gave Guy a straight look. 'If you're referring to the gossip, you, of all people, must know there is no substance to it.'

'Because you were—until so recently—a virgin you mean?' Guy suddenly looked very tired. 'You are very innocent, my dear. I don't seem to have changed that whatever else I may have done to you.'

She looked away in embarrassment. 'Do you have to make such—personal—remarks? It's hardly the time or the place.'

'As I've been saying all along,' he agreed equably. 'But if we are of one mind at last—at least on that—let us go.' He took her arm gently, but quite firmly. 'Now.'

She had no resistance left. She lowered her head meekly and went with him.

The car was the same sleek, powerful one they had used last night but his driving was different. It was, Robin thought, too fast, too aggressive, too abrupt, as if he were angry about something and was taking it out on the machine and his fellow drivers. When they stopped at traffic lights his fingers' ends drummed lightly on the steering wheel as he stared straight ahead. They did not speak.

He did not take her back to the flat. That was an enormous relief to her. Robin did not think she could bear the sight of the luxurious entrance hall, the knowing discretion of the porter, the steel and glass and pallid chintz which she could remember in every detail. And which recalled to her, in equally pitiless detail, exactly how abandoned she had been in his arms.

It soon became apparent that they were going out of London. They were on the motorway, passing the airport, ripping through the twilight at illegal speed.

She ventured in a small voice, 'Where are we going?'

'My house at Goring,' was the answer. He was almost absent about it, as if he was concentrating on other, more important, things than her presence or their destination. 'I've got a place on the river. My stepmother and sister use it mostly but they are in

London at the moment, so there's nobody there but the staff. I thought we'd better have some privacy. This could be a long session.'

'Oh!'

She digested that in silence. For a moment she wondered whether he intended to make love to her again and dismissed the thought almost instantly. There had been nothing remotely seductive in his manner this evening. If anything he had been slightly accusatory. There was certainly no sign of overwhelming attraction.

Robin sighed, pushing her hair back off her face. Well, there wouldn't be, would there? He was used to only the most gorgeous ladies and she had never been that, not even when she was eighteen and, so *he* had said, a wicked little witch who drove a man wild. She had had a certain schoolgirl appeal, she knew, that had all gone, overnight, after——

Robin suppressed her thoughts ruthlessly. That way lay danger. And anyway, Guy Gerrard was not interested in schoolgirls. If Marina was to be believed he liked his ladies elegant and intelligent and polished. So they did not try to cling to him when he was tired of them, Marina had added snappily when presenting Robin with this piece of information. It was at the start of their contract with him and Robin had entertained a tiny suspicion that Marina had, at one time or another, been one of the discarded ladies Guy Gerrard had tired of.

She looked at him now under her lashes. The beautiful profile, too arrogant to be alluring, was etched very distinctly against the soft evening colours of the landscape that flashed past. Robin thought ruefully that she could see what Marina had meant. He was not a man that a woman should involve herself with unless she knew very clearly that she could survive the end of his interest. Because when he wearied he would have no compunction in telling you so and little compassion in detaching himself from you; she could see that.

They were off the motorway now and driving through twisting lanes, overhung by innumerable leafy trees. The speed of the car did not decrease noticeably and Robin found herself surreptitiously clutching at her seatbelt. She said nothing, though a faint gasp escaped her lips as he swung the car with a violent bounce of its aristocratic springs, off the metalled road and round a seemingly endless curve of shingled driveway. Flung hard against the door by the violent movement, Robin shut her eyes.

The car straightened just as overhanging branches were brushing against the door panels with an ominous scratching sound. It accelerated, swung round again, this time almost in a full circle, and stopped. He killed the engine.

Robin opened her eyes cautiously. The car was standing on a sweep of gravel outside one of the finest Regency houses she had ever seen. It was not large but it was beautifully proportioned and the porticoed entrance was immaculate. Looking at the jewel of a house she realised, with a blinding flash of understanding, that this man was not merely a rich client but that he must be possessed of the sort of fortune that she had always thought died out after the First World War.

It alarmed her. She said abruptly, 'Why have you brought me here?'

His face, in the gathering dusk, was unreadable. He did not look at her. He was studying a rioting Zephirine Drouen rose that gave every sign of being about to push over a piece of insecure rustic trellis.

He said at length, coolly, 'To marry you.'

CHAPTER SIX

'You must be mad,' said Robin in despair.

She had been saying it for a hour and it seemed not to make the slightest difference. Guy smiled and nodded, almost seeming to agree with her, and then carried on implacably making plans for their marriage. He had even introduced her to his housekeeper, a cheerful and surprisingly youthful Portuguese woman, as his future wife.

'Look,' she said patiently, trying again, 'I don't want to marry you. I don't want to marry anyone.'

'I know,' he said composedly. 'That's what makes it possible.'

She gave an exasperated sigh and flung herself back on the swinging lounger in which he had installed her. They were sitting on what was, she discovered, the first of many lawns, looking across landscaped sward to the little sparkle of river to be discerned through the willows. The air was warm with the scent of honeysuckle and stocks. Bees hummed. In the distance the water lapped softly against the jetty. The lacy darkness of a summer evening had almost surrendered to night.

It was, thought Robin wryly, as near to Paradise as one was likely to come on earth. The only thing out of harmony with the warmth and peace and darkness was herself. Guy Gerrard, stretched out in an old-fashioned basketwork chair, a glass of whisky dangling negligently from between his fingers and his eyes half closed, looked as contented as a cat.

'*Why?*' she asked, for the umpteenth time.

A smile curled that lazy, sensuous mouth. She watched it, fascinated.

'Why not?'

'We don't like each other. We don't *know* each other, for God's sake.'

'In the strictly Biblical sense, we do.' His voice was dry. 'And I think it may be a good thing not to know too much about the person you are going to marry. As for liking,' he shrugged. 'What I know of you, I find admirable.'

Robin gave a half-angry laugh. 'Oh, you're impossible. You can't be serious.'

He took a draught of his Scotch before replying carefully, 'As you know perfectly well, I am absolutely serious. I need a wife and I need one fast.'

'But there must be hundreds of candidates,' Robin expostulated.

He laughed aloud at that, giving her a little mock bow. 'I am flattered. But no, there is not one. Apart from yourself, that is.'

'But there must be women you *know* . . .'

He interrupted, 'There are. And I know I could not live with them. Whereas with you it will all be a delightful journey of discovery.'

Robin stared at him. 'You mean you would really *rather* marry a stranger?'

He inclined his head again.

'I've never heard such nonsense in my life,' she told him roundly. 'I might be homicidal, a thief, a nymphomaniac, anything.'

Guy became even more amused. 'I see no homicidal tendencies. And people would not be letting you play with their rare and valuable *objets d'art* if you went in for pinching them. And we have established that you are no nymphomaniac,' he reminded her softly.

She flung him a defiant look, glad that the shadows

masked the flaring blush that he seemed to be able to induce at will and which, to her fury, she could not control.

'Yes, well. There are other things. Worse things probably. I might have a rotten temperament. I could make you very uncomfortable if I threw plates at you at breakfast,' she pointed out.

'Do you?' a faint interest sounded in his voice.

'Do I what?'

'Fling crockery at breakfast?'

She gave another choke of unwilling laughter.

'Not so far,' she admitted. 'But heaven knows what I would do if driven to it.'

'Ah. Yes. There's the rub. It is surprising the things we can be driven to,' he observed. 'The violence one would never have believed one was capable of. The stratagems one despises.'

Robin looked at him curiously. He sounded almost bitter, as if he was talking about himself. Was it because of his sister, she wondered. He had told her that that was why he had to marry. He had to have an older woman with the authority to take charge of young Laurel and, as he put it, shake some sense into her. His stepmother was on the edge of a nervous breakdown, largely because of her daughter's behaviour, and medical advice was that she had to be relieved of all responsibility for Laurel forthwith.

But Rose Gerrard was a conscientious mother; too conscientious, in Guy's view, or she would not have worried herself into illness over the antics of her only child. She would not stop worrying simply because Laurel went to live with her brother. She would not stop worrying even if he employed a full-time chaperon-companion. It had to be family. If Rose was to regain some measure of peace of mind she had to be induced to surrender charge of her daughter into the hands of some steady female member of the family. Guy had no other sisters. The aunts had declined categorically to have anything to do with the matter. So Guy had decided to marry and marry at once.

Now it sounded as if he regretted the necessity, as if he would rather have dealt with the thing straightforwardly without resort to subterfuge.

Robin said gently, 'Guy, there has to be some other way. Marriage is too final . . .'

'You know, you're extraordinarily unaware,' he told her, amused. 'Most women in your position would be thinking of ultimate divorce and counting up the sort of alimony they could expect. You just say that it is final.'

She drew back. She was shocked, really shocked, as if she had laid her hand on the fire or had the breath knocked out of her. It was true that she had not thought of divorce. She had not, so far, thought beyond talking him out of his ridiculous plan of marriage. But it made her wince to hear him speak so lightly, so scornfully, of women and their priorities.

She said quietly, 'I don't make promises I don't intend to keep.'

'There you are then,' said Guy triumphantly. 'Another excellent reason for marrying you rather than any other of my female acquaintances. There isn't one that I know of who could say that.'

She put her glass down carefully on the curlicued table beside her. He had given her a cocktail of his own devising, a drink which tasted innocuously of orange and cinnamon and was, she decided, a good deal headier than it seemed. It was making her forget all her fear, her inculcated mistrust of dominating, charming men, and luring her into imagining herself living with this man, taking breakfast with him every morning, making love with him, not out of one night's madness but as a looked-for expression of love and trust. For a moment the picture was piercingly sweet.

Then memory reasserted itself. There would be no trust to express. Suddenly the whole interview became unbearable. Somehow she must put an end to it, even if she had to tell some part of her closely guarded secret to do so.

Interlacing her fingers, she bent her head, not looking at him. She did not see, therefore, the blue eyes narrow and an altogether more serious, disturbed expression come over the handsome face.

In a low voice she said, with difficulty, 'You asked me—earlier—about the—well, the reasons for what happened last night.'

He murmured, 'I know about last night, honey. The reasons were pretty clear. I want to know the reasons for what happened to you before last night.'

Robin dipped her head in acknowledgement. Her smile was wry. 'Yes. I can see that. I suppose they're not—quite—the same thing.'

'They sure as hell are not,' said Guy forcefully. But when she jumped and looked up, startled, he moderated his tone at once and said, 'Go on.'

'It's all rather a long time ago,' she said hesitantly. 'You'll think I'm a fool.' She paused, martialling her facts, editing rapidly what she could afford to say without giving him enough to identify the old scandal. She knew she could not bear that.

'My father died when I was small. My mother married again. I never cared for my stepfather very much nor he for me. My mother spent most of my childhood begging me not to make trouble with him. He was a very——' she hesitated, looking for a word that would describe him and not reveal her unabated hatred at the same time '—dictatorial man. As soon as I was old enough I was sent away to school—to the relief of all of us.'

She paused, sighing. 'It solved the short-term
problem because it got me out of his way but it stored
up another one because it meant that he never got to
think of me as his daughter. I was just a visitor. There
were no taboos.' She was finding this more and more
difficult to say. His silence did not help, either. She
could feel the intensity of his concentration pressing
upon her. The old breathless pain in her chest that the
doctors, to a man, had diagnosed as psychosomatic,
came back now almost stifling her. She drew careful
breaths.

'When I was eighteen they—my mother and he—
made me come home. My mother said she wanted to
see something of me. And he——' the pain stabbed; she
pressed a hand to her side instinctively. 'My stepfather
was a famous man; not as rich as you but equally well
known; very handsome and popular and sophisticated.
I never thought——'

She was aware of him straightening slowly in his
chair. She knew his eyes did not leave her face. She
swallowed.

'He gave me a job. He insisted on doing so.'

And that was an understatement. She had not wanted
to work with him. She had begged not to. In spite of the
family tradition she had not wanted to be an actress.
The theatre, yes, that was a possibility; she would like
to design for the stage. She had told her mother so. She
did not want to act.

Her mother had not minded, not at first. It was
Francis who had been furious. Three generations of
actor-managers were being betrayed by the fourth, he
said. She owed it to her family, to her name, to her
father's memory.

Of course, later, she realised that Francis had seen in
her refusal to join the company a threat to its continued
existence and, hence, to his own. At the time she had

been too young and unworldly to detect his self-interest. When he spoke of duty she had been impressed. He made her feel guilty. And when at his instigation, her mother urged her to try—'Just one season, darling. You could always go to art school next year it it's really not for you. At your age you can afford a year, surely?'—she had agreed. It was a year to make her mother happy, that was the implication.

Only in the end it had not made her happy. It had not made her happy at all. How she must have wished, in the end, that she had let the rebellious daughter have her way in the first place.

Francis had wanted to star her at once. Never mind that she did not like acting, that she had no training, that there were better actresses out of work. The publicity value of having a Tyrell back in the company outweighed all that. Or so he said.

He had found, or had had found for him, an obscure Jacobean tragedy, a thing of blood and revenge with a murder every other scene and some intricate plotting by conspirators that must, Robin thought, have lost the audience well before the interval. But the poetry was marvellous. He dressed it sumptuously in ruby velvet and scarlet silk to contrast with the black-cowled monks who formed half the characters. It got excellent reviews.

Robin's part was not actually very large. She was killed off in her third scene by an irate husband having been found in a compromising position with the Duke. But before that there were two scenes—one in which the Duke first set eyes on her, one in which he tried to seduce and ended by raping her—which were a gift to any young actress wanting to shine.

And Robin had shone. The reviews were unanimous; in the provinces during the tour and then, when the play came to London, with one voice the

critics raved about the untried magic of this new
Tyrell. They spoke of the character's innocence, her
bewilderment, her anguish and showered Robin with
praise for simulating them. Her mouth twisted,
remembering. They had all been particularly impressed
by her terror in the rape scene. It had startled even
the jaded London critics.

Of course they did not know that by the time the play
opened in London, there was precious little acting
involved. The only professional skills Robin was using
by that time was projecting her voice and controlling
herself sufficiently not to run from the stage. Because
Francis was playing the Duke. And she was terrified.

At first she tried to talk to him; begged him to leave
her alone. He had laughed and said that everything he
was doing was necessary to the play, to her acting. For
a while she had even believed him. He could point to
the reviews to support him, after all. Did she think that
untrained actresses usually gave performances like that,
got reviews like that? No, she had him to thank and she
should bloody well not forget it.

But though Robin was young and, at that stage, very
innocent, she had not been a fool. It soon became
apparent that, whatever Francis said, and even
whatever he told himself, he enjoyed reducing her to
sexual terror; and that one day he would take it to its
ultimate conclusion.

She clenched her hands in her lap and went on with
resolution.

'One night he came to my room.' It had been her
dressing room, actually. Plenty of people came after the
performance. She had no obvious reason to resent his
presence, no legitimate excuse to throw him out. And
then the others had left.

'He had been drinking.' That was true. She had
smelled it on his breath. But it was not the drink that

had driven him. He was high on the adrenalin of a brilliant performance and long-delayed lust.

'There was a bit of a struggle.' She could not recall that silent battle, even now, without beginning to shake. It had been almost ridiculous; the two of them squaring up to each other in that untidy, over-heated cubby-hole of a dressing room. If it had not been so vicious it would have been the stuff of farce. He had lurched into a stool, knocked it over and brought her heavy velvet costume crashing down from its hanger. Knocking it away angrily he had lunged for her. She had tripped in the crimson folds that by then covered half the floor space. They had ended, struggling, among the tumbled skirts.

'He—I—He—' Her fingers were shuddering with tension, the knuckles of both hands white with it.

'Yes?' Guy prompted out of the twilight.

'He didn't rape me. Well, you know that. He threatened me.' She gave a long sigh as if she was glad to have said it and got it over with. 'And then my mother came in.'

But he would have no truck with evasion. 'How did he threaten you?'

'No,' said Robin on a high note of near hysteria. 'No please. I can't talk about it.'

In their fall a glass had been knocked off the dressing table. It was only a cheap thing. She had drunk some orange juice after she came off the stage. It had shattered. Putting a hand down to steady himself Francis had cut himself on a splinter. Cursing he had looked round; looking he had seen a large shard of shattered glass; he had picked it up.

Once again Robin felt the cold sweat of horror trickle down her spine. He had held it before her eyes, the jagged point gleaming. He smiled evilly; his Duke's smile. There was already blood on his hand from the accidental cut. He advanced the point to the corner of her left eye, just touched it against the skin so she felt it as a slight pin prick and said, 'Open your legs now, you bitch or——'

Robin gave a moan which she could not suppress. Unseen Guy's face took on a murderous expression but his voice was quite calm and academic when he spoke. 'If you haven't talked about it before you probably need to do so now, so that it doesn't fester any more. And you might just as well tell me as anybody.'

'As a sort of therapy, you mean?' she said drily, in spite of her distress.

'If you like.'

'I never believed in that sort of therapy.'

'It doesn't sound as if you have tried it.'

'No. I—no.' She hesitated, reluctant to share the experience which still sickened her.

'What have you got to lose by telling me?'

'Nothing, I suppose,' said Robin unhappily. She gave a little eloquent shrug and, bending her head, told him everything.

When she had finished he did not speak for a long moment.

'And your mother did *nothing*?'

She shrugged again. 'What could she do? Francis' story was that *I* had attacked *him*. It seemed plausible, you have to see that. He was the one with the scar, the blood. He said I had gone for him when he criticised my——' she stumbled over a word that would not give everything away, '——work. My mother already knew that we did not get on.'

'And it would be easier to accept than the alternative: that her husband could not keep his hands off her daughter,' Guy said coolly. 'Yes, I can see that. How old were you?'

'What?' Robin was confused by the unexpected bullet

of a question. 'Oh, I'd just left school. My birthday's in February. Half way to eighteen, I suppose.'

'*Christ*!' It was a soft, savage sound. 'Seventeen. He should have been shot.'

Robin said nothing. Her hatred for Francis could have corroded her life if she had let it. She had prevented it mostly by refusing to think about him. And by removing herself from her family and never seeing them or talking to them or communicating with them again.

'What did you do?'

'I left.' Running out of the theatre, through the dark, rainy streets, sobbing with fear and disgust, she had thought of nothing but getting away from them. She took nothing with her, not her passport, her birth certificate, no money beyond what she had in her handbag. That was how they had never managed to catch up with her. She had never cashed a cheque or retrieved a letter for her old self.

'Did you have friends? Somewhere to go?'

'One. An old friend of my father's.'

'Felix Lamont,' he said softly, half to himself. It was not a question. 'How much does he know of all this?'

Robin shook her head. 'Nothing. Well, I don't know how much he may guess. I was pretty—upset—when I arrived.'

'Yes,' he agreed expressionlessly.

'And afterwards I developed a sort of asthma. They said it was a nervous reaction. So the doctors may have told him something.' She shuddered. 'But I didn't tell the doctors everything. I couldn't. I felt so ashamed.'

'*Ashamed*?' He sounded incredulous.

Detecting scorn, Robin nodded, not looking at him.

'You were abused, misused and beaten up by a thug and *you* felt *ashamed*?' Anger licked through the smooth tones.

'I dare say you think that sounds very poor spirited,' Robin acknowledged, 'but you have—or rather I had— this gut feeling that somehow it is your fault. That if you'd been different, behaved differently, it would never have got to that pitch. You feel—culpable.'

'I fail to see why,' Guy said coldly.

'I don't think it's a logical reason,' Robin said, her voice dry. 'I can't explain it. I can only tell you what I felt.'

'I see.' He was playing with his glass, turning it round and round between his fingers, studying the movement with apparent absorption. He stilled it suddenly and looked up at her. 'So what was it that you felt last night?'

Taken unawares, Robin was thrown into confusion, drawing back into the comforting shadow of the hammock's canopy.

'I—I don't follow.'

'No? But it is quite simple. After years of chastity you suddenly resolve upon a change of policy. As I was the—er—beneficiary, I'd be glad to know why.' His voice was sarcastic. 'Did you cease to be ashamed all at once?'

Robin gave a choke of wry laughter. 'No. Quite the reverse. I'd never been so ashamed of myself in my life as I was this morning.'

'Then why?'

She thought about it. She had had plenty of opportunity; she had thought of little else all day. Yet she was still not sure of her answer.

'I think it was that I got angry,' she said doubtfully. 'Can you understand that?'

'Angry with me?'

'Partly. At least to begin with. But no, mostly with myself I think, for being such a cringing coward.'

He ignored the last sentence. 'Why were you angry

with me? Because I had the impertinence to employ you?' Guy demanded.

'No, of course not.' Robin was making a conscious effort to relax, to reply lightly. 'Even I am not that illogical. It was because of Lamia, our assistant.'

'Ah yes.' He leaned back in his chair again and his voice became a drawl. 'You mentioned her on the telephone. Accused me of frightening her, if I remember rightly.'

'Well, you did,' she told him.

He shrugged. 'Perhaps. She had only herself to blame. She had been mooning round me for days, getting in the way when I needed to concentrate. I didn't take kindly to being the subject of a schoolgirl crush so I thought I'd shake her up a little.'

'How?' asked Robin.

'Oh, a brief exposure to her idol's feet of clay. I let her back me into a corner and then got swept away by just enough passion to put the fear of God into her,' Guy said indifferently. 'It worked like a dream.'

Robin said in a quiet voice, 'I imagine my stepfather would have said much the same thing.'

There was a taut silence. Guy had frozen where he sat. She could see that from the unnaturally still line of his long legs in the shadows.

Then he said in a deceptively mild voice, 'Am I to infer from that, that you rate me as roughly the same sort of brute as your stepfather?'

'From my observation you have a lot in common,' Robin said, hating him as she recalled Lamia's pale face.

'Yes, I can see you might think that,' he agreed and, while she was still recovering from her surprise at the acknowledgement added in a steely tone, 'After all we are both men, which is what you really fear, isn't it?'

'I don't know what you mean,' she stammered.

But he was on his feet in a surging movement. Even in the darkness she could not be unaware of his anger. His whole body was tense with it.

'I mean that you are quite right when you call yourself a cringing coward, Robin Dale. I mean that you are afraid of men, of sex, of everything that makes you human. That's why there have been no boyfriends, no lovers to mess up your tidy little life. You were too damned scared.'

'I haven't wanted a lover,' Robin protested angrily. 'It's got nothing to do with being scared. If I'd wanted one I would have——' She stopped abruptly, seeing too late where her headlong defence was leading her.

'Would have reached out and taken one?' Guy supplied sweetly. 'I'm sure you would. As you did last night.'

'Oh hell!' said Robin with feeling, cornered.

'I think, don't you, that you've given me a number of scores to settle? I don't care for being used.' The words bit.

Robin made one last effort to defend herself. 'I didn't use you any more than you used me. We neither of us behaved particularly admirably.'

'But *I* wasn't telling any lies,' Guy said, quite gently. 'I found you attractive. I made it plain. I gave you every chance to decline gracefully if you didn't feel the same. I was not,' his tone hardened, 'offering to be some other man's whipping boy.'

'Don't!' said Robin sharply, jumping up.

It was a mistake. It was an incredible mistake because it brought her up short against him. His hands came out to steady her at that electric contact and instinctively she pulled against him.

'Don't!' she said again in a violent whisper.

He paid no attention of course. His hands, far from releasing her, lingered, travelled. Robin found herself drawn inexorably close. A faint breeze, curling up from the river, stirred the hair on the back of her neck. She shivered.

He misinterpreted the movement. Or perhaps he did not: Robin was never very sure how much of the shaking that started then was due to the evening air and how much to straightforward alarm.

'Afraid of me?' he said, his lips moving against her ear. 'So you should be.'

'W-Why?'

What had happened to their former understanding, Robin thought. It was unbearable, standing here trying to concentrate on what his oblique words meant when she was being wrought upon by those firm hands and the mothwing touch of his mouth.

'Because angry men are dangerous.' He touched his tongue to her lower lip and then leaned away from her, his voice becoming wry, self-mocking, 'And you have done nothing to placate me, have you?'

Robin stared up at him in the darkness, not understanding. He gave a sigh of exasperation. Long fingers closed about her jaw, tipping her face up to him, holding her unmoving as he bent his head.

'Pacify me a little,' he invited mockingly.

And then he was kissing her.

Robin gasped. She supposed he had kissed her last night—well, of course he had and she must have kissed him, too—but it could not have been anything like this or she would have remembered. It was an invasion, devastation, a ruthless taking of everything that she was. He knew that she wanted to deny him, was trying with all her being to deny him, and he swept it aside with an absolute mastery that both thrilled and appalled her.

He parted her lips without remorse. She tasted his tongue, the whisky he had been drinking, his teeth. She stiffened at the uninvited intimacy and he bit her lower lip, quite gently. A huge wave of sensual response hit her then and she shuddered. His hands tightened and his mouth became almost cruel for a second. Then he released her.

For a second they stood facing each other in the darkness like enemies. Robin's breathing was ragged. She felt dizzy, disorientated.

She said imploringly, 'Guy . . .' though she did not know what she was asking him for.

They were so close she could feel his chest rising and falling as he breathed. Did he always breathe so fast, so shallowly? She put her hand flat against his chest in a kind of wonder and he held it there, trapped.

'We are going indoors, you and I,' Guy told her coolly. In spite of the rapid breathing his voice was perfectly controlled. 'And we are going to continue the discussion where I should have started it. In bed.'

Robin cried out in wordless protest.

'Yes we are. You have quite a lot to learn about the differences between men. It will be my pleasure,' she saw his teeth gleam briefly in a wolfish smile, 'to undertake your education.'

'Let me go,' she said without any great hope of being attended to.

'And have you bolt for the fire escape, again?' He sounded amused. 'Figuratively speaking, of course. Not on your life, lover. This time you see it through till morning.'

'Y-You can't,' Robin protested, half horrified, half disbelieving.

'Can't what?'

'Keep me here against my will.'

His amusement deepened. 'Of course I can. That's exactly why I brought you here.'

She was afraid; deep in the core of her body she was

afraid of him, not as she had been afraid of Francis but as she had never been afraid of anyone in her life before. Because if he chose he could strip her down to the bare trembling bones of herself and then abandon her to the harsh winds of reality. She gave a little sob.

'You can't make love to me. Not again.'

'I can and I will,' Guy told her, laughing at her.

His hand closed about her wrist. He was drawing her away from the lea of the hammock towards the terrace, the open french windows, the flower-filled rooms she had glimpsed when they arrived.

'You wouldn't,' she said in a low voice. 'Not if I don't want to.'

Guy chuckled. 'If you didn't want to that would be another kettle of porridge entirely. Fortunately I don't have to consider that scenario.'

Before she knew what he was about he had swung her off her reluctant feet and into his arms. Alarmed briefly by the simple possibility that they might both come crashing to ground, Robin put her arms round his neck in a movement of pure instinct. He laughed under his breath.

In his room, or what she took to be his room, he deposited her carelessly in the middle of a large bed and turned away, ripping off his tie. Robin struggled up on to one elbow, amber eyes wide and pleading.

'Guy, please don't do this,' she said earnestly.

His laugh held a touch of recklessness. 'Why not? I have nothing to lose. Not with you.'

She closed her eyes, stabbed to the heart. He might just as well have told her that he did not give a damn for how she felt, that she did not matter to him in any way. It was surprising how much that hurt.

The shirt followed the tie as the blue eyes glinted at her.

'Aren't you going to take that yellow thing off?' He

bent towards her and pressed a hard, passionless kiss against her trembling mouth. 'Or do you want me to undress you, lover?'

'No!' She was horrified at the thought. 'And don't call me that.'

'Why not? It's no more than the truth.'

Robin flung herself off the bed and made for the door, terrified by the laughing implacability, by her own weakness. Guy caught her easily, spun her round and in one, fluid, expert movement, had her dress in a pool of honey silk about their feet.

Robin looked down at it, suddenly very still. His hands on her upper arms were firm but not bruising. He would not hurt her but he would not let her go. The breath caught in her throat and she raised puzzled eyes to his face, the shadow of her former panic still showing but dying away as he made no further hostile move.

Suddenly he bent his head and kissed one lifting breast in the gentlest of gestures. Robin's eyes widened.

He took her back to the bed and she went submissively, in bewilderment. The rest of her clothes were removed without haste, as if he savoured the task. Under his hands Robin found her body becoming pliant, yearning, full of a melting ardour which astonished her. When he placed a gentle kiss on her nipple a shaft of such acute desire went through her that she cried out, reaching blindly to press his head against her.

'So,' he said amiably, 'let us have no more nonsense about you not wanting to, hmm?'

Robin stared at him with drowned eyes, trying to focus her mind on what he was saying. It was hopeless. She could not concentrate under those lazy, expert caresses. He fingered his way down her spine teasingly and her lips parted in a soundless gasp, her lids drooping.

She had forgotten where she was, almost who she was. All she was aware of was wave after wave of exquisite sensation as, little by little, Guy coaxed her into passion and beyond to utter abandonment. There was not a square inch of her body that he had not kissed, she felt.

He gave a low chuckle of triumph. 'Do you want me?'

Robin squeezed her eyes tight shut. 'You know.'

'How can I know?' He pinched her gently, sensuously and her body reverberated with desire. 'Tell me.'

She moistened dry lips. 'I want you.'

'Then look at me and tell me so.'

She blushed. 'I *can't*.'

'Coward,' he teased and she felt his tongue on her lower lip, her throat, the throbbing tips of her breasts, tantalising with deliberate intent.

'Guy,' she moaned. 'Guy, for pity sake...'

'Then look at me,' he murmured against her skin, bargaining wordlessly with his wickedly unsatisfying touch.

'Please——' She was almost sobbing, not knowing what she was begging for.

'Of course.' He kissed her hip. 'Anything.' The fainting flesh of her thigh. 'Everything.' His hand followed his lips, warm and very sure. 'Whatever you want.' His touch was as light as rain falling on a cobweb; she could not bear it. 'If you will look at me.'

Shamefacedly Robin opened her eyes. Guy was leaning on one elbow above her, studying her face with concentration, a faint question in the depths of the azure eyes. She blushed, meeting them.

Naked he was beautiful, long limbed and spare, the powerful muscles no longer disguised by clothes. For all her arousal, Robin was aware of the stirrings of fear at the proximity of so much lithe animal power. He was so utterly alien, bone and sinew beside her softness, tanned dark where she was pale. And lying under his watchful eyes she felt like his prey, a small defenceless creature who had been hunted down and would now be sucked dry of life.

He saw the flicker of fear in her eyes and his lips tightened. Suddenly, as if he could not help himself, almost as if it were in spite of himself, he tipped her back among the pillows, tangling his hands in her hair, dropping his face against her breast so that she felt the rasp of his unshaven chin on her tender flesh.

And she felt more than that: she felt the hardness of his thighs, his unmistakable arousal, his weight that seemed to crush her fragile ribs and yet was not heavy enough, not close enough.

She flung her arms round him, binding him tight against her and as he moved, as they both moved, cried out to him a kind of anguish.

'So you will marry me.' His voice was low and panting but somehow he was holding himself off from her.

Robin shuddered and turned her head away on the pillow. He caught her hair and forced her to look at him, trapping her face between his hands.

'Marry me.'

She was terrified at the prospect but her body was in a tumult. The blood drummed in her ears.

'I don't understand you,' she moaned.

'You don't have to understand me. You have to marry me.'

He moved then, as if to withdraw and Robin cried out.

'Yes. All right. Anything. Guy, *please* . . .'

He smiled slowly and released her hair letting his hands drift along her limbs as he shifted, accommodated himself to her, moved finally to join their bodies. Robin made a high, choked sound and her body jack-knifed up against his. His mouth found hers, savagely, and they were caught up in a rhythm that Robin would have sworn she did not know but which overwhelmed her before she knew what was happening.

There were tears on her face, perhaps on his. He said her name brokenly. They clung together, moving wildly, searching each other's sweetness to the depths. Robin sobbed in her throat, dazzled. She heard him cry out, or thought she did. And the sun exploded behind her closed eyelids, shooting her out into the silent depths of space where there was only Guy and absolute, fulfilled, peace.

CHAPTER SEVEN

THE announcement of their engagement appeared the next day. So Guy Gerrard had not even waited for her consent before he sent the entry off to the newspapers. Not that Robin admitted that to anyone, least of all the columnists who immediately began to telephone her.

'This is frightful,' she said to Sally, after a particularly long and convoluted discussion with an American society journalist. 'I'll never get any work done today at this rate.'

Sally looked at her narrowly. She had not missed the fact that Robin, in spite of having her forthcoming marriage publicly announced and having been tenderly delivered to the office this morning by her attentive future husband, looked pale and strained.

'Refer them to Guy,' she suggested. 'He must be used to dealing with them.'

Robin's eyes flashed for a moment. She seemed about to speak but then, thinking better of it, closed her lips.

'Yes,' she said in a colourless voice and went back into her sanctum.

The truth was, though she was not prepared to tell Sally, that she had already had the idea of transferring all such calls to Guy. They had not spoken much this morning, constrained partly by the housekeeper's presence, partly by Robin's own overwhelming dismay at what she had promised. But he had touched her cheek lightly, understandingly as they were leaving the house.

'Don't worry, little one. Things will work out perfectly. You will see. Rely on me.'

It had consoled her. She gave him a half smile, ruefully acknowledging in silence that she was not sure that she could any longer rely on herself. She had truly thought that he had meant it, that whatever else might be wrong or precarious, he would support her.

It had been an appalling shock, therefore, to learn when she rang him later that he was already on his way out of the country.

'I'm sorry,' a cool-voiced assistant told her. 'Mr Gerrard has gone to Poland. He won't be back until the end of next week.'

At first she thought it was a mistake.

'No, he cancelled the trip,' she said positively.

Had he not told her that sometimes there were more important things which had to come first?

'Yes, he cancelled his flight last night. But it was only put off till this morning,' she was informed. 'I shall be speaking to him later. Can I give him a message, tell him who rang?'

'No,' Robin said dully. 'Thank you,' she added as an afterthought.

He had not even told her. She was so unimportant that, having deposited her at the door of the office this morning, he had completely removed her from his mind to the point where he had not even told her his travel plans. He had got what he wanted, which was a contract to look after his naughty sister, and then, like the good professional negotiator that he was, he had put it behind him and moved on to the next thing that required his attention.

Robin hugged her arms round herself as if in physical pain. She should have foreseen it, she thought, that access of indifference once he had got his own way. Francis had had it, too. It was not as if she had not had warning of the way men like that conducted their relationships. Why, oh why had she let herself be deceived?

Yet she had deceived herself. She had believed what she wanted to believe. He had made no protestations of love, offered her no fairytale ending. If she felt betrayed now it was not because he had reneged on his bargain but because she had made all the wrong assumptions: and on the basis of no evidence at all.

Robin gave a pained smile. Against all the odds she had been halfway to trusting him. Well, she had been taught a lesson. She would not make the same mistake again.

After that she handled the phone calls with composure. No, she had not known Mr Gerrard very long. No, they had not yet set a date for the wedding. No, he had not expressed a desire for her to stop working after they were married. (That, she thought with a faint touch of malice, would spike his guns if he subsequently decided that he wanted a home-bound wife.) Yes, she was very happy.

On the whole, though they asked the same questions, the columnists were not hard to deal with. They seemed friendly enough and not one of them failed to wish her well before ringing off. Even Xandra Leigh did not sound spiteful, just curious.

'And what does Dilly say about it all?' she asked.

Robin said, 'I'm sorry?'

'Dilly Cavanagh. She's been seeing quite a bit of him in the last few weeks. Didn't you see the photographs in *Starlight Magazine*?'

She was referring to a glossy quarterly that was given away free to homes and hotels in central London. Robin saw it, occasionally, though she did not read it. It was full of advertisements and horoscopes with the odd restaurant review. And a large number of society photographs, taken at parties that it was ingenuous to call private. Robin wrinkled her nose.

'No, I don't think I have.'

'Well, take a look,' Xandra advised her kindly. 'He's a nice chap but he can be a bit stupid about women. And if he thinks he will shake off the ambitious Lady Cavanagh with a little thing like an engagement to someone else, he's bats. You'd better watch out for her, Miss Dale. And I'm not printing that, don't worry. She's got a column of her own and I'm not looking for war.'

After a few more innocuous questions and what sounded like genuine good wishes she rang off.

Robin tried to put it out of her mind. She could not. She kept recalling that their conversations had been all about her. She could not remember him saying a word about his friends, his companions, his lovers. It was obvious that a man of his age and attractions would have former lovers. Anyway, it had been evident from the first that he was no celibate. Robin pressed pale hands against her cheeks at the memory of the specific evidence. But he had said nothing about any particular lady.

Yet, now she thought about it, surely Lamia had said that there was a new woman in his life; that that was why he was taking an increased interest in the house. If that were so, why on earth had he not asked this Lady Cavanagh to take charge of his rebellious young sister? It would have saved him the trouble of having to press-gang her, Robin. Then she bit her lip, half smiling. He had given every indication of enjoying having to press-gang her, she acknowledged. It was all very puzzling, not the least inexplicable thing being her own reaction to him.

By the end of the day Robin had a galloping headache. She felt as if her face was fixed in a rictus smile. She had received the surprised congratulations, faintly reproachful in the case of Bill de la Croix, of her colleagues. She had talked to Felix and listened to

Marina and given an interview to the press as to the manner born. All she wanted to do was to go home and shut her door against the world and listen to Mozart.

It was not to be. Sitting cross-legged on the mat outside her front door was a punk.

At first sight Robin was not sure whether the waiting figure was a girl or a boy. It had a crest of unnaturally black hair, stiffened with grease, ferocious patches of colour on the face and a skull and cross bones suspended from one ear. The clothes were black and fashionably rent below the knee. A number of what appeared to be bicycle chains were looped about the waist and down the arms.

Robin hesitated, raising her eyebrows. 'Did you want to see me?' she asked doubtfully.

The figure rose with surprising grace and came forward. It became apparent that the downy cheek under the warpaint could only belong to a girl and a very young girl at that. Robin's bewilderment increased.

'Are you Robin Dale?' the girl asked pugnaciously.

'Yes.'

'The porter wouldn't let me in. I climbed in through the storeroom window,' the girl said with a certain dispassionate pride. 'I wanted to talk to you. You're not going to marry my brother.'

'Ah. I see.' Robin smiled a little grimly. 'You must be Laurel Gerrard.' She extracted her key from her handbag and unlocked the front door to her flat. 'Shall we go in?'

Just for a moment the girl hesitated. Robin thought she had probably taken her by surprise. Then she collected herself and swaggered past into the flat.

'Let's go and sit down,' said Robin. 'I've been thinking about nothing but putting my feet up for the last hour. Would you like coffee? Or a drink?'

'Coffee's bad for you,' pronounced Laurel following

her into the sitting room and looking round with ill-disguised interest. 'So is booze. And I bet you haven't got any carrot juice?' she challenged.

'Er—no. I don't believe I have,' murmured Robin.

She sat on the couch and tucked her legs up under her. It served as a spare bed for when people came to stay but normally she kept it covered with a midnight-blue blanket and strewn with jewel-coloured cushions. She arranged the cushions comfortably behind her and watched her univited guest in some amusement as she prowled the room.

It was a comfortable room, a little untidy, full of books and pictures. An enormous bowl of lilac stood in the hearth, filling the room with the scent of summer. An eighteenth-century kneehole desk in the corner was covered in papers. A walnut case eighteenth-century grandfather clock stood in a softly lit alcove, its mellow ivory face and fine patina gleaming.

Laurel inspected it. 'That's nice,' she pronounced.

Robin warmed to her.

'Yes, isn't it? I picked it up in a sale, all battered. So I stripped it down and repolished it. And redrew the face on parchment. That was fun. I'd never done anything like that before. Fortunately the movement was undamaged. Do you like clocks?'

Laurel thought about it. Plainly it had not occurred to her before. 'Yes, I think I do. They're such straightforward things.'

Robin's smile was wry. That was perceptive of the girl. Or perhaps she knew too much about people who were not straightforward at all. She would be in a position to, with all that money; and a manipulative, charming brother like Guy Gerrard. She shifted sharply.

'Now, are you going to tell me why you don't want me to marry your brother?'

Laurel stopped prowling and sank cross-legged on to the forest green carpet.

'Oh, *I* don't mind whether you marry him or not,' she said magnanimously.

Robin's thick, expressive brows rose. 'Then why did you say what you did, that I wasn't to marry him?'

Laurel shrugged. 'That you *wouldn't* marry him,' she corrected. 'Because you won't. My mother will stop it.'

'What?'

Robin was genuinely taken aback. Had he not said that it was entirely because of Rose's health that he had to get married and take Laurel off her hands? He had not been lying, surely he had not been lying. He had seemed so concerned.

Laurel had clear blue eyes rather like her brother's. They met Robin's with absolute candour.

'You don't know anything, do you?' she said with adult pity.

She rummaged in her back pocket and produced a much sat upon packet of cigarettes which she offered to Robin. Robin shook her head. Laurel extracted a cigarette, lit it with what looked like an incongruously expensive lighter, and wrapped her arms around her knees, resting her chin on the top of them as she smoked. She regarded Robin unwinkingly.

'I'm having a fight with my mother,' she announced. 'That's why I'm here. I thought it would be a good thing to spike her guns.'

She drew on the cigarette, regarding the glowing tip meditatively.

'There's a conspiracy, you see. Between my mother and Guy's mistress.' The clear little voice was expressionless. 'Rose wants me off her hands so she can pretend she's twenty years younger and get herself another man. And the Cavanagh wants to marry Guy.'

Robin jumped. 'Lady Cavanagh?'

The small nose wrinkled in disdain. 'The first Lady Cavanagh. Douglas divorced her and found himself somebody nice on the second try. Douglas,' she added grudgingly, 'isn't bad.'

'Oh,' said Robin faintly, not finding Laurel's revelations very reassuring.

'So Rose got her tame quack to tell Guy that she couldn't take the strain any more and he had to get married and give me a stepsister-in-law. I,' the voice grew gruff and there was a suspicion of a flush under the cosmetics, 'made a bit of a boob by pushing off to Italy with an Undesirable.' She gave a sudden grin, making her look like a naughty schoolboy. Robin remembered, startled, how young she was in spite of her sophisticated talk. 'I get along with Undesirables: they don't muck about. Though this one was a mistake. And the Cavanagh homed in on Guy the moment he got me back from Italy.'

She grimaced, flicking ask inaccurately in the direction of a large blue glass ashtray.

'You were there?'

'I was listening,' Laurel said, unashamed. 'I reckoned it was my business. Rose was wringing her hands and talking about psychiatry.' She snorted. 'She's mad about doctors. And the Cavanagh was saying I needed a firm hand and a little polish.' There was blatant horror in her voice. 'They *both* kept on saying that it was no good Guy just giving me a home: I needed a woman's influence.'

Robin felt a great relief. So he had not lied to her. When he said that Rose had insisted her daughter needed another woman in the family, he had spoken no more than the truth. Here was the corroboration.

'But where do I come into all this?'

Laurel leaned forward. 'Oh, that was Guy's idea. He's no fool, my brother.' There was a sneaking admiration there. 'He must have seen that one could not marry a creature like the Cavanagh.' Laurel's voice became thoughtful. 'I expect she's fantastic in bed, though,' she said reflectively, 'all snakelike and slinky, you know.'

'Laurel!' protested Robin, shocked as much by the indifferent tone as by what she had said. She sounded suddenly very like her brother in one of his less amiable moods.

Laurel looked surprised, then disgusted. 'Oh, don't you think I ought to know about sex? Am I too young? Would it make you more comfortable if I pretended it didn't exist?'

'It would make me more comfortable,' Robin said with asperity, 'if you kept your reflections on your brother's private life to yourself.'

Laurel sniffed. She did not apologise but Robin had the impression that she was slightly abashed.

'Well, the Cavanagh's not house-trained. One could not *live* with her whatever her other talents might be like.'

Robin flung up a hand in silent protest. Laurel subsided.

'I'm just explaining,' she said in an injured voice. 'Guy said that they were exaggerating and he and I would get on perfectly all right on our own. He knew what they were up to, you see. He'd already moved out of the flat when Rose asked the Cavanagh to stay.' She became gleeful. 'They must think he's stupid, or something. The Cavanagh just moved in and set herself up in the bedroom next to Guy's. So he packed a grip and went to stay in Sue Temple's flat: said that they would be better able to entertain without him asking for quiet all the time. The Cavanagh,' she added with satisfaction, 'was furious.'

Robin felt that she ought to stop this. If Guy wanted

her to know these things he would tell her. It made her
uncomfortable to receive a present of them from his
half-sister.

She said, 'Why are you telling me this, Laurel?'

The girl looked down.

'It didn't seem *fair*,' she said at last. 'With Guy
pushing off all of a sudden like that and the Cavanagh
phoning all her friends in London telling them about it.
I thought I'd—redress the balance, if you know what I
mean.' She gave Robin a sudden, blinding smile. 'I'm
glad I did. I like you.'

'Thank you,' said Robin absently. 'What do you
mean—telling them about it?'

Laurel shrugged her expressive shoulders. 'She's been
ringing all her mates, the columnists and people. Rose
has been doing it, too. Saying that the engagement is
only temporary.'

Robin was surprised and faintly bewildered. 'But how
can they account for that? Why the announcement?'

Laurel flushed then. The bright eyes clouded. 'It's not
very nice.'

'What isn't? Oh, what they are saying you mean. No,
I imagine it wouldn't be.'

Robin waited expectantly; not in vain.

'They're not actually *saying* it, you know,' Laurel
said wearily, as if she was long familiar with the
technique. 'Just hinting. It makes it sound more
feasible. That's what they do to Guy about me.'

'And?' prompted Robin.

'They say that he got drunk and fell into bed with
you,' Laurel blurted out, not looking at her. 'And as
you're not his usual type, not "one of us",' she
mimicked what Robin took to be her mother's languid
tones, 'he's got a conscience. Or you're blackmailing
him. Whichever they think the other person will
swallow.'

Robin sat very still.

'Why does that make it temporary?' she demanded between stiff lips.

'Because he'll break it off when he comes to his senses,' reported Laurel. She flushed. 'Or when, if, that is, he is sure that you're not pregnant.'

Robin gasped, flinching.

'I'm sorry,' said Laurel miserably.

There was a painful pause. Robin felt Laurel's words penetrate slowly, like slime. She felt unclean, wretchedly vulnerable, filled with distaste for the people who could say such things. Her mouth twisted bitterly. Not that she should be surprised. Had she not heard it before, from her own mother? 'It's your fault, you led him on, you're a slut, you're lying to protect yourself.'

Her skin crawled. She felt smirched.

Laurel said with uncharacteristic timidity, 'Are you angry?'

'Yes,' said Robin.

It was true. A great tide of rage was building up. How dare they? How *dare* they? The yellow eyes began to smoulder.

Laurel said, 'I wanted to get in touch with Guy and warn him. But they wouldn't give me his phone number and that bitch of a secretary wouldn't tell me where he is staying in Warsaw. So I came to you.'

'Very sensible,' Robin approved, taking hold of herself. It was not, after all, this child's fault. She was a rather unlikely champion but, in contrast to her elders, she at least meant well. 'I suppose I should thank you.'

'What are you going to do?'

'I'm not sure,' Robin confessed. She thought for a moment. 'I can tell you what I am *not* going to do though, and that's give people any reason to believe that your mother and her friend are right.'

Laurel's eyes gleamed appreciatively. 'Great,' she

said. She stood up, stretching and limbering. 'Well, the first thing you'd better do is get yourself an engagement ring. I'll pinch it for you.'

'I beg your pardon?' said Robin, not sure that she had heard aright, even from this unconventional creature.

Laurel grinned. 'Guy's mother's,' she said succinctly. 'It's in the safe along with all of Rose's stuff. I know which it is because my grandmother showed me once.' Her eyes clouded a little. 'She said it was bad luck and that was why Guy's mother died young but I don't believe that. And it's gorgeous: a yellow sapphire set in diamonds.' She looked at Robin appraisingly. 'It will suit you.'

'I can't do that,' Robin expostulated. And as Laurel began to protest, said firmly, 'No, I can't and you must see that I can't. It may be all right for you to go rummaging through your brother's safe—though I doubt it, myself—but I can't. Nor can I be a party to it.' She added with a gleam of mischief, 'I'm sorry to be a nuisance. And I do, truly, appreciate the offer.'

Laurel hunched a shoulder. 'Oh, you're obviously as hung up on property and ownership as the rest of them.'

'I'm hung up, as you put it, on not being thrown in jail before Guy comes back from Poland,' Robin said wryly.

Laurel grinned with one of her lightning changes of mood.

'That would be *marvellous*. He'd kill Rose. Or throw her out, anyway. Make her buy her own flat and never let her near Willow Grove again.'

Her eyes took on a predatory gleam and Robin said hastily, 'Laurel Gerrard if you have me framed I will personally see that you go back to school and stay there.'

Laurel was quite unmoved by the threat. 'You'd have to find a school to take me first. Guy can't.' She chuckled. 'But I won't frame you. I'll tell you what, though. I'll go with you to my Uncle George's charity concert tomorrow night. And,' she added with superb assurance, 'I can make sure that we get photographed together. "Sister and wife-to-be making friends"; that sort of thing.'

Robin was amused and rather touched. 'You would make a good politician,' she told her visitor.

'Yes, I think perhaps I would,' agreed Laurel, pleased. She moved to the door. 'I'd better be going. I'm meeting the gang at Flannel's. I'll give you a ring about Uncle George's. Oh and Robin——' she paused, a little awkwardly. 'I know it's difficult, but I think you'd better let Guy know what's going on. When he rings you.'

She left. Robin saw her out, watching the odd little figure skip down the quiet corridor with a mixture of emotions. Uppermost was bleakness.

Laurel had not asked about her relationship with Guy. She had clearly assumed that anything her mother and Lady Cavanagh said was a lie but she had not gone beyond that. How could Robin tell her that it was altogether too close to the truth?

Above all, how could she tell a child who was already too sophisticated for her years that the woman who was about to marry her brother had not the slightest hope or expectation that he would telephone her from wherever he was tonight?

CHAPTER EIGHT

ROBIN was to find that Laurel spoke no less than the truth when she said that her mother and Dilly Cavanagh were doing their best to spread the rumour that her engagement to Guy would not last long. The papers next morning, at least those that bothered with such things at all, were full of it. Bill de la Croix came and sat on the corner of her desk and read her extracts.

' "Millionaire's abberation",' he read with relish. 'I say, Robin, that's a good one. Have you ever thought of yourself as an aberration before?'

'Never,' she assured him, peering over his shoulder. 'That's a horrible photograph of Guy. It makes him look like a thug.'

Bill's look was dry. 'He can be thuggish sometimes, you know, my sweet. Far be it from me to cast aspersions on the love of your life, but it has been known for him to play dirty in his business life.'

Robin shrugged. She knew that he spoke the truth and it worried her but she was not going to admit as much to Bill.

'Business is a dirty game. Go on, Bill, What else does it say?'

' "Glamorous Guy Gerrard, long time breaker of hearts, has announced that he is to marry at last. The lucky lady is interior decorator Robin Dale, late twenties, not one of his recent escorts. Robin, a working girl, says she hasn't known him long and doesn't intend to give up her career for marriage. On-going friend Lady Dilly Cavanagh agrees that it is all very sudden. 'I haven't seen Guy since it happened,'

says Lady Dilly, thirty-three. 'He can be so impulsive.'"
Phew.' He lowered the paper. 'She sounds like one prize
bitch. She makes it sound as if she turned him down
and he took up with you on the rebound.'

'Yes,' agreed Robin absently, leafing through the
other papers. 'Rather clever, isn't it?'

Bill looked at her curiously. 'Don't you care?'

'About what the papers say? Not a lot. I'm pretty
furious with that Cavanagh woman, I'll admit.'

'You must be very much in love with him,' said Bill,
sighing.

Robin frowned. 'How do you make that out?'

He smiled sadly. 'Robin my love you are almost
neurotic about your privacy. If you don't mind being
plastered all over the gossip columns for him, you must
really have given your heart in a big way.'

'You may be right,' she admitted, trying to sound
casual. 'What about the others?'

'All more or less the same. Here, you look at them.
"Guy Gerrard's Secret Love", "The Last of the
Bachelors Meets His Match", "Mystery Woman To
Wed Millionaire".' He pushed them across the desk
towards her. 'Not an original thought or phrase
between them and somebody has clearly been pouring
poison, too.'

'Even Xandra Leigh?' asked Robin, disappointed.
She had liked the sound of the journalist on the
telephone.

'Which one's she?' Bill riffled through the papers.
'Oh, the *Despatch*. No, that's nicer than most.' He read
it out. ' "One of London's unknown beauties has
caught Guy Gerrard's discerning eye." There you are,
middle of the page.'

Robin skimmed her eye down the printed column. It
was all standard stuff, listing his business interests, his
leisure activities and naming the women with whom his

name had been linked in the past. She was coming to know them all by heart. It made it all the more peculiar that he should have insisted on marrying herself.

'Have they been round asking for a photograph yet?' Bill enquired.

She raised her head from contemplation of the article, startled.

'No. Do you expect them to?'

'With someone who is as big news as Gerrard, I'd say it was a certainty.' He grinned at her. 'Got some pretty holiday pics in a bikini, my sweet? That's the sort of thing they like.'

Robin laughed. 'They wouldn't like *my* holiday snaps then. I'm insulated to the gunnels in thermal underwear on the ski-slopes and completely unrecognisable.'

'They'll probably send out the photographers then,' Bill said tranquilly. 'I'll tell Sally to stand by for a siege, shall I?'

'Stop teasing me,' she said, throwing her memo pad at him. 'I'm not royalty.'

He fielded the pad neatly, one handed.

'You might just as well be if you're determined to marry Gerrard.' He gave her a mock-ingratiating smile. 'Sure I can't persuade you to change your mind? Swap the prince for a humble woodcutter, lady?'

She stood up. 'Get out,' she ordered, laughing. 'You've had enough fun at my expense today. Out. I want to get on with some work.'

Bill grinned and backed out, pulling an imaginary forelock.

He was replaced, almost immediately by Sally Jackson, bearing an enormous bouquet of flowers. She peered round the edge of it, feeling her way carefully. Robin looked up in amazement.

'What on earth . . .'

'Your best beloved,' said Sally with restraint, 'has

been destocking the florist.' She found the desk and let the flowers go with a sigh of relief. 'Lamia has looked out every vase we've got and is pretty certain we shall need some more. I told her to go and get what was necessary from Goodes and put it on the account.' She surveyed the flowers with disfavour. 'You didn't tell me he was an extremist.'

Laughter bubbled up in Robin, in spite of her doubts. 'I didn't know,' she assured Sally, her eyes dancing. 'He gave no sign of it. I thought he was quite normal.'

'Well, those flowers are definitely over the top,' pronounced Sally. 'And I suppose you've got thousands at your flat as well. *Men*! They never think.'

She marched out before she noticed Robin's sudden stricken look or absence of reply. The truth was, of course, that Guy had no idea where she lived. On both occasions they had met he had found her somewhere else: once here, at the office, once at Felix Lamont's.

Robin touched a finger tip against a pollen-dusted daisy petal. There were flowers of every description in the bouquet. Guy could not have specified anything particular. They were a gesture, a public claim, there was no private message in them.

There was, however, a small pasteboard card, written in round schoolgirl writing, presumably by someone from the flower shop. Robin opened it.

It said simply, 'Don't forget, Guy'. Robin frowned, turning it over between her fingers. What did it mean? Was she not to forget their bargain? Well, he had made sure of that by publishing the notice of their engagement. In fact, that probably qualified as one of what Bill had called Guy's dirty tricks.

Or was she not to forget that it was a private arrangement? Was this a cryptic way of warning her that she must not let slip the real circumstances of their engagement. She sighed and went back to her desk. She was beginning to feel drained. She had done almost no work and her in-tray was piled high with things that could not await Marina's return.

She buzzed Sally.

'I am not in,' she said. 'And I need a sandwich lunch.'

'I should think you need a stiff drink,' said Sally, but she laughed and promised to bar the door.

And that was how Robin got through the next week. By dint of coming in to work early and leaving late she not only caught up with the work, she effectively gave the photographers the slip. In this she was aided by Sally who told them all that there was no truth in the rumour that Miss Dale had gone to stay in Mr Gerrard's country house. The photographers, almost to a man, left for Willow Grove at once. It was a brilliant ploy and one that Robin was very nearly certain had been suggested to Sally by her future stepsister-in-law.

Laurel had appointed herself Robin's guide and mentor through the dark labyrinth of Guy's friends and family. After Uncle George's concert, there was a cousin's garden party to which Laurel frogmarched Robin on Saturday afternoon. Neither Rose nor Lady Cavanagh was in evidence in either gathering. Laurel, however, who had modified her appearance only slightly in deference to Robin's company, was very evident and, as she remarked with satisfaction, much photographed.

Robin laughed at her but she was grateful for the girl's friendship. She was growing increasingly nervous about what was going to happen when Guy returned, as he was due to do at the end of the next week, and full-scale war broke out in the Gerrard household.

Rose, reported Laurel with unconcealed delight, was furious and would not have Robin's name spoken in her presence.

It was all distinctly alarming and not helped by the

fact that the two people who knew her best, Marina and
Felix, found the situation extremely amusing. Felix had
not stopped chuckling since the day he heard, from
what Robin could gather. And Marina, telephoning
from Tuscany, said she was delighted and, darkly, that
Robin and Guy deserved each other.

It was with relief, then, that Robin left the cousin's
garden party, said an affectionate farewell to Laurel,
and walked home through the sunbaked London
streets. Dust lay on the pavement like chips of
diamonds. In spite of her cool georgette dress and
strappy sandals, Robin felt desert-hot.

Her flat was an oasis of cool. She closed the door
behind her with a sigh, leaning against it wearily. Her
flesh seemed to drag at her bones.

'You look exhausted,' said a low, amused voice. 'It's
just as well I've got some champagne on ice.'

Her eyes flew open in blank bewilderment. She stared
at him for an unnerving second as if she thought he was
a ghost, or some figment conjured up by a fevered
imagination. She shook her head, not believing it.

Guy was here. *Here*, in her private place that he did
not know existed. Here, days before he was expected,
lounging on the sofa looking impossibly handsome with
one of her books open beside him,

Robin said in a voice like sandpaper, 'What are you
doing here?'

The mobile eyebrows rose at her tone but he did not
comment, merely swinging himself to his feet and
smiling at her, 'The porter let me in. He half expected
me, I gather. He certainly wasn't surprised when I
suggested that I wait for you up here.'

'I, however, did not expect you,' Robin said precisely.
She found she was shaking as she came away from the
support of the door; the realisation made her furious.
'You scared me silly.'

Guy bent to kiss her lightly on the cheek. 'Not you. You aren't silly and you don't scare easily. Though you look tired, I'll admit. What have you been doing? Shopping for your trousseau?'

Robin gave him a look verging on dislike. 'Of course not. I've got more sense than to shop on a midsummer Saturday afternoon when all the world and his wife are doing the same. I've been to a garden party at some sort of cousin of yours. Laurel,' she added gloomily in explanation, 'insisted.'

His eyes gleamed with laughter. 'Yes, I've been hearing about your growing intimacy with my sister. It must be very wearing.'

'Laurel,' said Robin pugnaciously, 'has been very kind and friendly.'

'Oho. Curiouser and curiouser.' He took her chin between finger and thumb and turned her face to the light to receive his inspection. 'Is it my appalling sister—notwithstanding her kindness and friendship—who has put the shadows under your eyes?' he asked interestedly.

Robin's lashes flickered revealingly. She detached his hand. 'I've been working hard.'

'And that worries you? Because, to be quite frank with you, lover, you look worried to death.'

She said between her teeth, '*Don't call me that.*'

Guy's eyes flashed but he said in a tolerant voice, 'No, you're not very loving at the moment, I'll give you that.' He paused before adding, 'Is it the press? Marina told me they had been giving you a bad time.'

'Marina?'

'Your senior partner,' he explained, mock solemn. 'I had to ring her to get your address. Which reminds me, why aren't you in the telephone book? It must be a disadvantage for an interior decorator to have an unlisted number. I found it very inconvenient.'

Robin was very still. Then, with an effort, she shrugged. 'I didn't want clients ringing me up at all hours. They have the office number; there's an answering machine there.'

She had, of course, been terrified that it would be Francis who would find her out and start calling her. The name was no great invention, after all. Robin was what Felix had always called her, from a child, when he said she reminded him of the garden bird. Dale was her maternal grandmother's name. Oh yes, Francis could have found her out easily enough and if he had done there would have been nothing to stop him beginning those old tormenting, fearsome games all over again. He had enjoyed her fear. He would have enjoyed terrorising her from a distance.

She paled at the very thought. Guy saw it. He said abruptly, 'Is there something you haven't told me? Something I should know?'

For a moment, Robin was tempted. He was so forceful, so comfortingly competent. She could not imagine him living in the dread of shadows as she had done.

But in the end she could not tell him. The habit of privacy was too engrained. Besides, she was not entirely sure of him. He had blasted into her life with the force of a rocket and she was still reverberating from the impact. He was compulsively attractive: he could make her tremble with passion. He made her laugh. She respected his brain and his energy. Perhaps she liked him, she was not quite sure. But she knew she did not yet trust him.

If she was keeping her own counsel on some things, so too was he. Robin was sure of it. There was something in his eyes when he looked at her, something speculative and oddly serious which she could not interpret and which he did his best to disguise. And there was that business of his claim that he preferred to marry a stranger. It was arrant nonsense and he had not done much to pretend that it was anything else. But he had not told her why he really wanted to marry her.

At length she shook her head decisively. Her hesitation had given her away, of course. Guy's face darkened.

'God, you're set in concrete, aren't you? What do I have to do to get through to you?' he said bitterly.

Robin's eyes widened in alarm and confusion. She shifted nervously.

'I—I don't understand.'

He passed a weary hand through his hair, the grey wings at his temples very apparent against the tanned skin.

'No, I don't suppose you do. God help me, I'm not sure that I do, any more.' He sat down on the couch and gave her a straight look. 'I think we're overdue for a talk, lover. Stop glowering at me and come and sit down.'

Robin moved warily to the chair opposite him and sat, with as much composure as she could manage. She leaned back against the upholstery, stilling her hands in her lap with a conscious effort. Guy noted the distance she had put between them in one eloquent flicker of the blue eyes. His smile was a little twisted.

'Maybe you're wise. I'm not noted for keeping my hands off you.'

She flushed unhappily, looking away.

'We have, nevertheless, got to get a couple of things sorted out. Such as, first of all, are you going to marry me?'

That brought her startled gaze back to him, parting her lips in a gasp.

'But I thought—I mean you said——' She broke off

in confusion. 'You made me promise. Don't you want to marry me?'

It was surprising how hurtful that possibility was. He waved it aside.

'That is not what we are discussing. And I made you promise, if you remember, under duress.'

Robin bit her lip. 'I remember,' she said.

'But you didn't think that that was unfair?' Guy pressed her, his eyes keen. 'You didn't think of going back on it the next day?'

Robin's eyes flashed. 'How could I? You had already announced it to the world. In fact, you must have sent that notice in before you announced it to me,' she said with resentment.

'Quite.' Guy looked amused. 'So you could have denied it. Told the papers it was a hoax. Published a retraction. Why didn't you?'

Robin bent her head. 'It never occurred to me,' she said in a shamed voice. 'I am very stupid.'

'Possibly,' he said. 'Possibly. Or there again, it might be that marriage to me was all you really wanted.' He paused expectantly. 'What do you think?'

'I don't know,' Robin said at last. 'I honestly don't know. I—a week ago I'd never thought of marriage. It was something that happened to other people, not to me. I didn't want it or not want it; it simply wasn't my—oh, my area of activity, if you like.' She paused, thinking.

'And now?' prompted Guy.

'Now? I'm not sure.' She gave a wry grin. 'I've grown used to the idea, though. Between the newspapers, and your sister, and that bank of flowers you sent me, I don't seem as if I can remember a time when I didn't expect to marry you.'

She looked up at him, smiling, expecting him to share her sense of the irony of the thing. He was quite inscrutable though, the brilliant eyes half hidden under drooping eyelids. Her smile withered on her lips. She had that odd sensation again of being excluded from something important, something that affected herself.

She said uncertainly, 'Doesn't that make sense?'

'Oh, it makes sense,' Guy acknowledged. 'Not perhaps quite the sense I had hoped for but it does have its own logic.' He sounded bitter. If it had not been ridiculous, Robin would have said he sounded hurt. 'The truth of the matter is that you don't know whether you want to marry me or not but you're quite happy for me to make the decision. Disappointing in an independent lady, but there are bound to be throwbacks to the old submissive days, I suppose.' He leaned back among the cushions, stretching his long legs in front of him and giving her a lazy smile as he went on softly, 'So if you don't know whether you want to marry me, do you know whether you want to go to bed with me or not?'

Robin's hands knotted involuntarily. The silence between them lengthened unbearably as she sought for something to say, her brain seemed to freeze so that she could not string two phrases together. And Guy was no help at all, sitting there watching her in mockery.

'I—can't answer that,' she said at last, helpless under his inspection.

'No?' He was sarcastic, soft-voiced. 'Why do you think that is?'

Her hands began twisting themselves in her lap. She felt like a schoolgirl under interrogation for some misdemeanours. She resented the feeling, but it was none the less powerful.

'I don't know.'

'Perhaps I can be of assistance.' He raised an inviting arm from the cushions and crooked a finger. 'Come here.'

Among her own personal things he was the invader, hated and feared and alien. Yet he was still heart-stoppingly attractive. And the long body on the sofa was not really an intruder because he had been there, in her imagination, every night since she had returned from Willow Grove.

Her mouth was suddenly dry. Robin swallowed, moistening her lips with the tip of her tongue.

'Come *here*,' Guy said, suddenly hoarse.

She could not move. He was tense as a coiled spring, watching her with unwinking hunter's eyes. The space between them was a chasm she dared not cross. The gold-flecked eyes widened, mirroring exactly her trepidation.

'Why do you look at me like that? Do you think I'll hurt you?'

She shook her head dumbly. She did not know the answer to that question. Had she not been asking it of herself all week?

In one lithe, contained movement he was beside her, kneeling in front of her chair, gazing intently into her face as if he would search out her feelings one by one and extract them into the light of day. Robin drew back instinctively, her eyes falling away from the intensity of his.

She was aware though of the bitterness that touched the sensual mouth at her movement. The skin of his face was taut, the high cheekbones stood out as if they had been etched in acid. The whole aspect was one of tension verging on pain. Robin did not understand it.

'Is that my answer, then? You want me—a little—but you are more afraid that I will hurt you again.'

She was stung to protest. 'You didn't hurt me——' She looked up, saw him briefly anguished and was lost.

She raised a hand to his cheek very gently, amazed as his breathing deepened, grew more rapid. She felt very calm. Holding his eye steadily she tipped her head in mute invitation of his kiss. Guy bent his head and took her offered mouth with shattering force.

Later—she did not know how much later nor had she any very clear idea of what had happened in the interim—the doorbell pealed, high and intrusive. They were lying on the carpet. Guy was shirtless and tousled. Robin's pretty skirts were tumbled in a froth of georgette and satin petticoats and she had lost her shoes. The dainty fabric-covered buttons had come undone to the waist and the bodice was pushed away from one creamy shoulder.

At the sudden noise they both froze. Guy's mouth moved against her collar bone.

'Don't answer it,' he urged softly.

The bell pealed again, harder. Whoever was at the door must be leaning on the bell push. Guy sat up, grimacing, running a not altogether steady hand through his hair.

Robin fumbled with her buttons, delicately flushed. He reached out and displaced her fingers, finishing the task himself.

'There. Respectable again,' he teased, drawing his hand away down the soft fabric-covered curve of her breast.

Robin shuddered with a little eddy of desire so strong that she had to shut her eyes. His fingers paused, lingered at her aroused nipple.

'Robin, when you look like that, I could—' He cut it short and dropped his hand like a stone as the bell rang again in a shrill imperative. He stood up, reaching down a hand to her. 'Come on, lover; see who your visitor is and get rid of him.'

She opened the door still in some confusion. Her dress was buttoned and straightened but her hair was tumbled, her feet bare and her eyes wide and dazed still.

And nobody looking at Robin's mouth could doubt that she had just been thoroughly kissed.

The woman to whom she now opened the door stared straight at her mouth and obviously drew the correct conclusion.

'Miss Dale? Are you not alone?'

'Er—no,' Robin admitted. 'That is, yes I am Robin Dale. How can I help?'

The woman was striking, not quite beautiful but arresting. She was casually, expensively dressed and perfectly made-up. Even in the heat she looked as cool as an ice cream.

'I am Dorothy Cavanagh,' she said now. 'We haven't met.'

'Ah,' said Robin, horribly conscious of bare feet and no make-up. 'No, we haven't. Can I do something for you?'

Lady Cavanagh submitted her to one comprehensive look that said, more clearly than words, that Robin was not a candidate for her service.

She said coolly, 'On the contrary, Miss Dale, I came to do something for you. Give you a little advice in fact. I understood you would be alone here this evening.' A look of malicious amusement crossed her face. 'That was the impression my little friend Laurel had, anyway. She said you told her you were going to go home and go to bed. Presumably she just assumed that meant alone?'

The woman's spite was so obvious that Robin recoiled. Lady Cavanagh gave her a vulpine smile.

'These children are so innocent.' She shrugged. 'And I imagine she thought that in the circumstances, even though Guy was away ...' She let it trail away meaningfully. 'I won't keep you a minute though, Miss Dale. Can I come in?'

Robin struggled with herself. She did not want the

woman in her home. On the other hand she did not want to trade insults on the doorstep, which was clearly the only alternative. Lady Cavanagh, she recognised, was not going to go away until she had said her piece. Reluctantly, she stepped back.

Lady Cavanagh swept past her in a cloud of 'Magie Noire'.

'What a charming place,' she said graciously. 'Of course, you design for a living, don't you? I must say, it shows. Perhaps you would do some work for me sometime?'

Robin inclined her head, not answering. The sitting room, she saw in one comprehensive survey, had been tidied. In particular, it had been emptied of Guy's overpowering presence. That was both a relief and a slight anxiety. She could guess where he had gone and the thought made her uneasy. She was not sure that, once again in charge of her feelings, she wanted to spend another night in his arms.

She was a little *distraite* as Dilly Cavanagh began to talk. It was clearly a prepared speech and had been rehearsed until it was fluent. Robin focused on only a few of words.

'Suitability' was one. 'Acceptable' was another. Robin brought her concentration back to the conversation with an effort.

'I'm sorry,' she said politely. 'I don't think I understand.'

Lady Cavanagh's laugh tinkled charmingly. 'There you are, my dear. That's exactly what I mean. Guy, in his position, needs a wife who can pick up these little nuances without having to have them spelled out for her.'

Robin's heavy brows met. 'Guy's position?'

Again that laugh, like marbles falling on concrete.

'He's more than just a successful businessman, you

know.' A sigh. 'No, I suppose you don't know, you poor child. He's in the forefront. He is a spokesman for the business community all over the world. And of course, there's the family background, the wealth. He has to be *seen*; he has to be a patron of the arts, for example. And his wife will have to deal with all that.'

For a moment Robin was assailed by amusement. The golden eyes lit with laughter and she said solemnly, 'You mean he needs a wife who is already expert at spending money.' She paused and added in a thoughtful tone, 'And that you have a better record in that than I.'

Dilly Cavanagh drew in her breath in a hiss of pure venom. Her face grew ugly.

'At least I'd keep my side of the bargain,' she said. 'Not go falling into bed like a slut with someone else the moment he was out of the country.'

Robin flushed but said steadily, 'I think I will forget that remark, Lady Cavanagh.'

The other woman took an impetuous step forward. 'Forget all you like,' she sneered. 'He shall know about it. And he won't like it, you know. He's possessive. He may be a cold fish but what he has he keeps and he keeps it to himself. I think you've just made a big mistake, Miss Dale.'

'On the contrary.'

It came from behind them in level tones. Both spun round. All the colour left Dilly Cavanagh's face, leaving the skilful maquillage cruelly highlighted on her papery skin.

'*You!*'

Guy gave her a small smile as he strolled forward. 'I think the mistake is yours Dilly.'

He had used the interim to get rid of the rest of his clothes and had acquired for his own use the old towelling robe that Robin kept hanging in the bathroom for occasional overnight guests. It was too

large for her by several sizes but it was not big enough
for Guy's broad-shouldered frame. The front gaped
open to reveal a tanned chest with its dusting of curly
dark hair; and though it was belted properly enough it
came no lower than his thighs.

Robin blushed, embarrassed at his assurance, at the
other woman's dismay, at the kick of desire that she felt
immediately in the pit of her stomach at the sight of
him. When he put his arm lightly round her body and
drew her back against him she did not resist, but she
stiffened.

Lady Cavanagh said in a disbelieving whisper,
'You're in Poland.'

Robin could feel him smiling. He dropped a light kiss
in her hair. 'I couldn't stay away any longer.'

His hand moved possessively on the rounded curve of
her hip. Seeing it, the woman's eyes flickered. Robin
was filled with an enormous compunction. Guy was
giving no quarter. She remembered what Bill had said:
oh yes, he could be ruthless. Dilly Cavanagh's livid,
ravaged face bore witness to it.

She tried to move away from him but at once that
caressing hand was like a steel claw, holding her still
with very little display of effort.

'You'll regret it.' Lady Cavanagh, like Guy himself,
was ignoring Robin. She glared at his unmoved
expression. 'A girl from nowhere. No background.
What do you know about her?'

It was no less than she had said herself, thought
Robin, pained for her. To expose herself like this Dilly
Cavanagh must be really in love with him. She, Robin,
could only shiver at the thought of being so much in love
with someone that you did not care to what
degradation you put yourself to try to keep him. And
whatever Laurel might say about Dilly Cavanagh, she
was not bitching or lying now. She was pleading her

case with straightforward fact. And, like Robin before her, she got nowhere: Guy had made his mind up and was not going to debate the point.

Guy said quietly, 'That is our business, Dilly. Forgive my plain speaking.'

She stared for an instant and then, flushing angrily, turned on her heel and strode from the flat, banging the door behind her.

CHAPTER NINE

THE moment the door banged shut Robin moved away from Guy's body. He did not try to restrain her again. His hands fell back to his sides and he watched her, not speaking.

'Was that really necessary?'

He shrugged. 'What would you have preferred?'

'You could have been—kinder.'

The lop-sided smile dawned, driving those indentations down his cheeks that made him look so formidable.

'You feel kindly disposed to her after what she said to you?'

Robin realised, with a sort of horror, that he was genuinely unmoved. He had been the woman's lover, he had left her without so much as a word of warning, if Laurel was to be believed, discarding her for a new lady and a new life and he had no compassion at all. Robin shivered.

'I would have thought you owed her that much,' she said with difficulty.

His eyebrows rose. 'I? Owe Dilly Cavanagh? My dear girl, you're raving. Where is the debt?'

'She sank her pride, coming here like that,' said Robin, frowning, distressed. 'She looked desperate.' She raised her eyes swiftly to his. 'You must have felt something for her once.'

Guy smiled, not very pleasantly. 'The only feeling I have ever had for Dilly Cavanagh is one of profound irritation,' he said coldly. 'If she wanted to make a fool of herself by coming here that was entirely her own business. I don't give a damn, except in so far as she upset you.' His voice hardened. 'Even you will allow that I could not permit that.'

'I suppose not,' she said almost inaudibly.

'But she's managed it anyway, hasn't she?' Guy was resigned. 'Damn the woman.' She flinched. One day he would speak like that about her, Robin, to whoever was the new incumbent of his affections. This marriage would not last any more than any affairs of his had lasted. Perhaps less. Had he not talked of divorce the very night he had made her agree to marry him? More than that, had he not made his basic indifference very plain? She could hear him saying, as if he were saying it again now, in this room, 'I have nothing to lose. Not with you.' She felt very cold.

He said harshly, 'Don't look like that. The woman is poison but she is nothing to do with you and me.'

Robin smiled wryly. 'You mean you keep her in a separate compartment?'

He shrugged. 'If that's the way you want to look at it.'

'Which compartment do you keep me in, Guy?' she asked quietly.

His eyes narrowed. There was a little silence. 'Now what do you mean by that?' he asked softly, at last.

She met his look straightly. 'I mean that you went off to Poland without a word, without telling me, even, that you were going. I mean that you left me to deal with all the reporters without a word of warning. I mean that you never telephoned me while you were away. You just left me to get on with it.'

Guy pushed his hands into the pockets of her robe. His face was unreadable.

'Did you want me to telephone you?'

'That's beside the point . . .'

'No, it isn't,' he interrupted. 'You've made your attitude to myself more than clear. I did not think a gratuitous telephone call would be welcome.'

He was wilfully misunderstanding her, Robin thought. She said indignantly, 'You could have *warned* me.'

His mouth twisted. 'Of what? That I would be away? Or that you would miss me?'

She gasped, startled and silenced.

He said quite gently, 'Don't you see, if I'd done all the things you think I ought to have done, you would never have found out that you missed me?'

Robin said nothing. She was remembering with appalled clarity that Bill de la Croix had said that she must love Guy very much. She had dismissed it at the time. Now she began to wonder if both men had seen something that she had not.

She stared at him, her expression hostile.

He cursed softly. 'Dilly would be delighted with the result of her intervention,' he remarked. 'I'll go, if that's what you want.' He paused. 'It is, isn't it?'

Without speaking, Robin nodded slowly, her thoughts in turmoil. He laughed briefly, harshly, and went out.

Robin found her shoes and a comb which she ran through her hair. In the hall mirror she looked unnaturally pale, except for the rosy mouth that was still faintly swollen. She touched her fingertips to it tentatively. They were trembling. She turned sharply away from the mirror.

When Guy emerged it was as if the last half hour had not taken place. He looked tidy and composed. In contrast to her dazed tension, he looked relaxed. He kissed her cheek casually as he passed.

'Have an early night. I'll ring you tomorrow.' He smiled. 'So you won't start feeling neglected again.'

She nodded, without speaking. He dusted a kiss along the quivering lower lip and left.

Her early night was a disaster, she tossed and turned in her too hot room. Half the time she longed for him, a deep, primitive longing which shocked her. The other half she was afraid.

He was a stranger. More he was an alien, out of her orbit. She did not know how to take his careless laughter, or his passion that looked like tenderness and could be switched off in a second. What did he want of her? What was even more unnerving, what did he think he had already got?

In the end she got up and tried to work. The wild-eyed, flushed lady in the bathroom mirror looked scarcely capable of work, thought Robin with bleak self-mockery, but if she concentrated she would do it—and put Guy Gerrard, at least temporarily, out of her mind. Only then she caught sight of her mouth again, and gave a bitter laugh. Before she knew Guy Gerrard she had never thought of herself as sensual. But it was there now, the sensuality she had not been aware of, and she could no longer deny it.

Eventually, by dint of several cups of coffee and a complicated assignment, she succeeded in pushing to the back of her thoughts the memory of Guy Gerrard and the unwelcome change he had wrought in her. But to banish him entirely was impossible.

When he rang, at eleven, she was tired but calm.

'I thought you might like to come down to Willow Grove,' he suggested in a neutral tone. 'I've got rather a lot of work to do but we could have lunch and you could swim and bask afterwards while I put in a couple of hours at my desk.'

Robin contemplated her own desk in amusement. Whatever else he was, the experienced Mr Gerrard did not seem to have much appreciation of the fact that his lady of the moment might have quite as much work to do as he had himself. She told him so.

He laughed. 'Are you calling me a male chauvinist pig?'

'Very, very subtly,' Robin assured him in amusement.

'Well, apologise.' Guy's voice was warm. 'I never doubted your professional dedication. I merely paid you the compliment of assuming that you were too well organised to work at weekends!'

'Unlike yourself?' Robin teased him.

'No, I never work at weekends either. This time is special because I whizzed through my meetings in Poland and I have all the paperwork, which I should have done there, still to catch up on.'

Robin's brows twitched together. She had come to know him well enough to be certain that he would not skimp on his business obligations except for something really drastic in his private life. Funny how she was so positive of that, although in many areas she did not know him at all. But he must be desperately worried about Laurel if he had cut short his trip abroad because of her.

She did not let any of her feelings show in her voice, saying carefully, 'Would we be on our own?'

Guy gave a soft laugh. 'Do you mean am I going to jump on you again?'

'I—No, I . . .' said Robin flustered. She had genuinely not meant anything of the sort. She had been trying to discover whether his stepmother and Laurel would be at the house by the river.

'No, I don't imagine you need to ask,' Guy's voice was dry. 'It must be patently obvious that I jump on you every chance I get.'

Robin made a strangled sound to which he paid no attention.

'But on this occasion you are safe. My grandmother

will be there. My father's mother, so she's Laurel's grandmother as well. She has expressed a desire to give Laurel a talking to, which I believe she is administering now. I said they had better have some non-aligned company at lunch or they'd murder each other. So I shall have to go down anyway.' He hesitated and then said in a tone that she would have thought, if it had not been ridiculous, was almost diffident, 'It would be nice if you would come, too.'

'To hold your hand?' she asked, relieved to get the conversation back to a conventional, friendly level. 'All right, I'll join the peace keeping force.'

He laughed, that warm, friendly sound that made her melt and want to reach for him. 'You're a brave woman, Robin Dale. I'll pick you up in forty minutes.'

Afterwards Robin dated their public relationship from that afternoon. It was the first time she had been anywhere with him as his future wife and she was surprised at how easily she found the part came to her. Standing in the circle of a possessive arm as he introduced her to his grandmother, she felt shy and proud and protected as if they were real lovers, instead of fiercely attracted strangers with a diplomatic alliance.

The attraction was there all the time, of course, none the less burning for having to be curbed in the presence of others. Even when Mrs Gerrard left they were not alone, for Laurel was still there and friends and neighbours dropped in for a drink in the garden. There seemed to a convention that if Guy was home he kept open house on Sunday evening. And the constant friendly stream of people was almost more than Robin could bear.

She knew Guy felt the same. That was another of the things that she knew about him, she thought wryly, looking across the terrace to where he was listening cheerfully to a couple of ageing neighbours. He was propped against a low wall, his ankles crossed, and he looked absolutely relaxed and absorbed. But meeting his gaze, she saw that he was aware of the same tension as herself, the same spiralling impatience to be alone.

Her lashes flickered, recognising the fellow to her own suffering. She saw his eyes darken. He turned and put his glass down very carefully on the wall beside him as if his hand had begun to shake. Robin's mouth went dry. She wrenched her gaze away and transferred it resolutely to a woman whose name she could not remember who had introduced herself as a friend of Rose's.

'So delightful that dear Guy is going to take the plunge at last,' she was saying, her eyes avid. 'And all so sudden, the papers said! Quite a romance.' She looked doubtful. 'Though I'm sure I've seen you before, somewhere? You're sure you haven't been going out with Guy in secret for ages?'

Robin shook her head amused. 'No, truly. It's quite as sudden as the papers say.'

'One look and you both fell headlong! How splendid! And so rare too, though in dear *Guy's* case it is most understandable.'

She was saying, Robin thought without animosity, that she had no idea what he could see in such a nonentity. She decided to amuse herself.

'Thank you,' she said solemnly, deliberately misunderstanding. 'Though I think Guy's pretty stunning, too. But then I suppose I would.' He had come up behind her and she gave him a little mischievous smile over her shoulder, 'Wouldn't I, darling?'

He had heard the conversation and his eyes were dancing. 'I hope so.'

He put both hands on her hips and drew her back against him, setting a casual kiss on the curve of her shoulder. Robin, for all her awareness of their guests, could not prevent a sweet, deep shiver, as if they were alone. Their companion watched them, her eyes narrowing.

'And we've never met before?'

'Never,' Robin assured her, smiling, trying not to be distracted by the firm hands which were not withdrawn.

'It's extraordinary. I could have sworn . . . Perhaps you have a double, Miss Dale? Or may I call you Robin?'

'Please do,' she said blithely. 'But no double, I am afraid. At least, not that I've heard of.'

The woman was still dissatisfied. 'I know I've seen your face somewhere.' She snapped her fingers impatiently. 'I'll ask Dilly Cavanagh. She's got all sorts of records at her office. I pride myself on never forgetting a face. It'll come to me.' She smiled at them both. 'And then I can introduce you to your double.'

Guy said softly, 'Don't bother on my account, Shushu. I've found the only girl *I* want. I don't care if she has ten doubles.'

Robin's throat was so full of emotion she could hardly speak. Oh dammit, when he talked like that, when he *looked* like that, she loved him so much.

Suddenly realising what she had thought, Robin froze. Love? *Love* Guy Gerrard? Was she out of her mind?

The woman he had called Shushu was moving away, wishing them well, smiling brightly. Robin looked after her blankly.

She could not, surely she could not, have been so stupid as to fall in love with him. The whole situation was fraught as it was, without a complication like that. It must be physical attraction. Her untutored body had responded to him with fervour and she had mistaken that for love. Desperately she tried to tell herself that it was a mistake, a momentary aberration, a slip of the tongue almost.

She was so close to him that he could not avoid knowing something of what she was feeling.

He said, for her ears alone, 'Something's wrong. What is it? *Does* she know you?'

Robin disengaged herself.

'Not as far as I am aware,' she said with constraint. 'I suppose we could have met.'

There was no mistaking the absolute lack of interest in her voice. Guy's eyes narrowed as he watched her.

'Then what was it?'

'What was what?' fenced Robin, stepping away from him.

'Something upset you. Don't try to deny it. I felt it. You went rigid.'

'Oh—that was nothing alarming,' said Robin with difficulty. He was too compelling in his charm, the blue eyes dark with what looked like concern. 'I—I just remembered something I hadn't done. I shall have to do it tonight,' she continued, improvising desperately. 'I mustn't be late back.'

When she had finished there was a little silence, as if she had said something quite different; as if she had issued a challenge, almost, and it required his whole attention.

He said evenly, 'I thought we would stay here overnight and go back to town in the morning.'

She shook her head in sharp rejection of the idea. 'No, that won't be any good at all. I have to finish this tonight and get in to work early tomorrow morning. Marina's away, you know.'

'Yes,' he said without expression. 'I know. Very well, if that's what you want. We'll go whenever you like.'

Robin was startled. She looked round at the people still on the terrace. There were ten or a dozen left.

'But your guests . . .?'

He shrugged. 'They're not all mine. Some of them are

my grandmother's and she has left. Some of them are Rose's, like Shushu Devane, and Rose wasn't here at all this weekend. Laurel will stay tonight. She can see them off the premises and lock the doors after them, if that's what you're worried about.'

Robin was embarrassed and it showed. 'No, of course that was not what I was worried about,' she said crossly. 'I just don't want to be a nuisance, that's all.'

She glared at him, seeing his ironic half smile. 'Well, I don't. I'm not so desperate to get back that I have to drag you away from your guests. Just as long as I get back tonight, I will be all right. Otherwise, we can go whenever suits you. What do *you* want to do?'

His lids dropped lazily but under them the eyes were smouldering. He studied her for an unnerving minute, not speaking.

Then he said, 'I, as you very well know, want to drum my friends out of my house, lock my sister in her room and carry you off to bed. Where,' he added with a flicker of humour, 'I would make love to you to such effect that you would not get up and go to work next week, let alone tomorrow morning.'

Robin flushed violently. She bit her lip.

'But the plan clearly does not appeal. Let us think no more of it. I will just tell Laurel we are off and I am entirely at your service.' He gave her a little mock bow from the waist. 'As a chauffeur, of course,' he added mockingly.

He turned and left her. Robin was speechless. The blood coursing in her veins reminded her that her every nerve responded to him.

It was chemistry, she told herself, pressing the palms of her hands together in a vain attempt to calm herself. Nothing more than chemistry. It was only because she had chosen to lead such a restricted life that she had not felt like this lots of times before. Most women of her

age had done, must have done. And Guy certainly had.
It had nothing to do with the once and everlasting love
that the poets talked about.

The thought of Guy's previous lovers steadied her. It
put the thing back into context to some extent.

In the darkness of the car on the way back to
London she summoned up her courage and said, 'Guy
could I ask you something—personal?'

He gave her a swift unsmiling look in the shadows. 'If
you don't have the right to, I don't know who has,' he
said a little grimly.

Robin looked down at her hands.

'I—you may think it's none of my business. Don't
answer, if you don't want to. It's just—I was wondering
about—well—your life before, I mean . . .'

Guy took pity on her. 'You want to know about the
women before you,' he said.

It was not quite the way Robin would have put it.
Presumably, the women to whom he had made love on
previous occasions had been neither strangers nor
prospective mentors for his erring sister. But as a
shorthand it would do.

'Yes.'

'What do you want to know about them?'

'Not their names or anything like that,' Robin
flinched from the thought of him telling her a list of
names, ending, of course, with Dilly Cavanagh. 'Just,
oh have there been lots, have they been important, did
you want to marry any of them?' A thought struck.
'You haven't married any of them, have you?'

'Good God, no.' He sounded blank. 'Didn't you
know that?'

She shook her head.

'You really are very—unusual,' he said thoughtfully.
'One forgets.' He drove for a moment in silence. She
thought he was marshalling his facts. Then he said with

an odd urgency, 'Robin, I'm not a child nor a saint. I've taken the opportunities that came my way; most of them, at least. I never expected to marry but I've never hurt anyone. Can you understand that?'

She said slowly, 'It sounds very simple put like that.'

Guy groaned. 'I knew it would come to this in the end,' he said, half to himself. 'You're too innocent.' He paused and then said gently, 'The world has changed, you know. Things that my grandmother finds shocking happen all the time today. I'm not responsible for the change; I just live with it as best I can. And, as I say, I've never deliberately hurt anyone in my life.'

Robin thought of Lamia's desperate little face as she protested, no, really, Mr Gerrard had not offended her, she had been a fool. She thought of Lady Cavanagh, hungry-eyed and hysterical, sinking her self-respect to hunt him down.

She said in a low voice, 'And not deliberately?'

Guy made a sharp movement, quickly stilled. 'Robin, we all do things we're sorry for, cause pain we didn't intend. I'm not alone in that.'

She was relentless. 'How often? To how many?'

It was turning the knife in her own wound but it had to be done; before she lost hold of common sense completely and was lost in the depths of unexpected, unwanted and unrequited love.

'How many?' she repeated, wincing at her own question.

He raised a hand from the steering wheel and thrust it through his hair almost violently.

'*God*, Robin . . .'

He set both hands on the wheel, bracing himself almost. The speed dropped noticeably as if he were taking the car and himself in hand at the same time. When he spoke again it was in a controlled voice, deliberately calm.

'I cannot pretend that you are the first woman in my life. I wouldn't even try. I like women. I enjoy their company. I have the usual biological urges. Occasionally—I stress, *occasionally*—in the past that has come, briefly, to be something more.'

'How much more?' asked Robin in a hard little voice, aware that she was inexplicably hurting herself with her persistence. 'How much more?'

A quick impatient glance. 'There have been two serious relationships, if that's what you want to know. One when I was at university—with a much older woman. One later.'

Dilly Cavanagh, thought Robin in a daze of pain. Oh, why had he not married Lady Cavanagh? And why was she, Robin, asking these questions when she so much did not want to know the answers?

'And the others? The ones who weren't serious?'

Guy drew a long breath. When he spoke his voice was careful, even gentle. 'These things happen, lover. Maybe not to you, but they do to a lot of people. Perhaps even the majority these days. I'm not some sort of eighteenth-century rake. I don't go around seducing the unwilling or raping the innocent. They happened by mutual agreement.'

'And nobody got hurt?' she mocked.

'Nobody was intended to get hurt,' he said, still patient.

'That wasn't what I asked, though.'

His composure began to crack. 'God, I don't know. How can I? Perhaps once in a while somebody misunderstood, misinterpreted . . . Hell!' He broke off. 'Look, if they got hurt, I didn't forsee it and I didn't intend it. Doesn't that count for anything?'

Robin thought of Lamia and poor, aggressive Dilly Cavanagh.

'Not a lot,' she told him coolly.

'You're not long on charity, are you?' Guy asked. 'But since you're so intent of accusing me, answer me this: what have you done in your life? How many men have got ice burns off you, my sweet?'

'Nobody,' said Robin positively.

'No? What about the tame puppy prowling outside your office the day I came to collect you? He wasn't sure where he stood with you, but he sure as hell wanted to punch my face in for taking you out.'

Bill de la Croix. And yes, Robin knew that he wanted her, in his quiet self-effacing way. He had made it more than plain and she had ducked the issue. But she was not going to admit that to Guy Gerrard.

She said, 'I don't know what you're talking about.'

He shot her an unsmiling look. 'No? Well, what about old Lamont, then?'

'*Felix?*'

'Yes, do you know what I'm talking about there?'

'Felix is an old friend,' Robin said stiffly.

'An old friend who looks after you like a hawk protecting its young?'

She smiled instinctively. It was an apt description.

She said in a calm voice, 'There is no point of comparison. Felix and I are very fond of each other but he is not in love with me.'

'My dear girl,' Guy said, his tone heavy with irony, 'you have not the faintest idea of who is in love with you. Or how much you might be able to hurt them.'

Robin was startled and slightly affronted. 'But I don't give them any encouragement . . .'

'Precisely.' He pounced on it with satisfaction. 'You don't mean to hurt them. It doesn't stop you doing it, though, does it?'

She said heatedly, 'You're just trying to wriggle out of it. When *you* said that sometimes people got hurt, what you meant was that other people got hurt. The ladies involved. Because you didn't, did you?'

He said curiously, 'Would you rather I had?'

'At least it would prove you were human.'

Unexpectedly he gave a wry chuckle. 'I'd have thought you'd had proof and to spare of my humanity.'

She glared at him in the darkness. 'I know what you want. I know the lengths to which you'll go to get it. That's humanity at its lowest.'

There was a nasty little silence.

'You hit hard when you get going, don't you?' Guy said at last on a long breath.

Robin shrugged, not answering.

'And I ask myself why,' he went on in a meditative tone. 'I've been pushing as hard as I—well, I've been pushing for days without getting poison spat at me. What happened tonight to change things?' He went still. 'It was when we were talking to Shushu. It was something she said. Tell me!'

'It wasn't,' she said in an unconvincing whisper.

He said very quietly, 'Robin, I know you've been hurt. I keep reminding myself of it. And the way we met didn't help; I can see that. I want our marriage to work. I will take care of you, I promise. And I will be——' he hesitated '—reasonable. I won't ask for more than you can honestly give. But I think I have a right to know all the important factors in our relationship. And I think you're holding out on me.'

She shook her head in the darkness.

'Does Felix Lamont know?' he asked with apparent irrelevance.

She said again, 'I don't know what you're talking about.'

'No? Then let's drop the subject.' He drove in silence for a moment before saying in an odd wrenched voice, not at all like his usual laughing tones, 'But if I find

that you've kept something important from me—
something you've confided in Felix Lamont—I swear I
will make you regret the day we met.'

Robin said almost inaudibly, 'You make yourself
very clear.'

'And there's nothing you want to tell me?'

'There's nothing I want to tell you,' she agreed dully.

For an instant he held himself absolutely still, as if he
had received a wound. Then he sat back in his seat,
flexing his shoulders, his hands taking a looser grip on
the wheel. 'Then let's go home,' he said without
expression.

And the powerful car speeded up into the night.

CHAPTER TEN

AFTER that things became both easier and, obscurely, more alarming. Guy left her alone a good deal, claiming to be very busy. He did not, however, leave the country again. Every three or four days he took her out to dinner somewhere public, often with other people. He seldom telephoned her—his secretary made all their appointments to meet—and they were never alone.

Robin felt as if she were living in limbo. She continued to work as if her life depended on it, spending long hours at the drawing board. She usually arrived at the office before anyone else and, except when she was going out with Guy, stayed late into the evening after everyone had left.

Returning from Tuscany, Marina found that all the tasks she had delegated to Robin had been completed along with a few more. She went through her papers with an increasingly black frown. At the end of her first morning she pushed the files away from her, buzzed Sally asking her to book a table at the Italian restaurant round the corner, and went in search of Robin.

She found her in their main gallery talking to a prospective client. The woman was middle aged and, from the quality of her unseasonable silver fox jacket, wealthy. She was also hesitant and apparently bewildered by the breadth of choice of furnishings available to her. Robin was talking, guiding her gently. It was exactly the sort of job that was usually Bill's or Tony's prerogative. Marina's frown became thunderous.

When the client had left, clutching her sketches and

pattern swatches, Marina said grimly, 'I don't know what the hell you think you're doing, Robin but you can't go on like this. You'll wear yourself out.'

Robin was surprised. Marina was not noted for her tenderness for the health of her staff. Nor, having a great deal of energy and enthusiasm herself, was she given to detecting that they were overworking. Robin's eyebrows rose therefore.

'By helping a client choose a carpet?'

'By helping thirty clients choose half a hundred different bits and pieces,' retorted Marina. 'Have you any idea of the work you have got through while I've been away?'

'Aren't you pleased?' Robin was amused. 'How ungrateful of you, when we have all been working so hard.'

'Not the others,' snapped Marina. 'You.'

'The others have been working very hard, too.'

'Yes, I can see they have,' she said impatiently. 'But they've been working sensibly. While you—you must have been racing like an engine on a speed circuit. What's got into you, Robin? It's not a race, you know.'

Robin shrugged, smiling, not answering.

Marina went on, 'And it looks to me as if you've given up eating as well as sleeping and taking time off. You're as white as a sheet. Well, I'm not having it. I'm going to take you out and feed you and you will tell me what in God's name has been going on.'

Robin blinked. 'Going on?' she echoed.

'Look,' said Marina patiently, 'I didn't leave you in charge so you could work yourself into the ground. You've never done so before. I thought you could handle it.'

'Are you saying I haven't?' Robin was mildly affronted.

'No. Not exactly.' Marina hesitated and then said, 'We'll talk about it over lunch. Get your bag.'

The Italian restaurant was one they patronised fairly frequently when they had clients to entertain at lunchtime. The head waiter found them a quiet table behind a plant-strewn pillar and brought them a carafe of ice-cold wine without asking. Marina poured two glasses, took a long heartening draft and then sat back in her chair, looking at Robin over the top of her elaborate spectacles.

'What I really want to know,' she said slowly, 'is what you have been doing to my darling Guy.'

Robin winced and looked away, swirling the wine she did not want round and round in its long glass.

'I don't know what you mean,' she said at length.

'No?' Marina was dry. 'But I'm told you got engaged to him while I was away?'

'I—er—Yes.'

'And you'd never met him before the day you went down to his house in Mayfair?'

Robin shook her head.

'So you just met—took one glance at each other— and pouf! Nothing will do but legal matrimony.'

Robin felt the blood creep slowly up into her cheeks.

'That's not quite what happened,' she began with difficulty.

But Marina interrupted her. 'Near enough, though.' Her eyes narrowed. 'What are you up to, Robin?'

Her colour deepened. 'What should I be up to?'

'Oh, stop fencing with me. I've known you too long. You don't like men, do you? You never have. You've kept them at arm's length for ten years. You've had no lovers, not one. So why, now, have you decided on Guy Gerrard?'

Robin could not answer. Marina continued to scrutinise her. The waiter arrived to take their order which Marina gave in an absent voice. She bent down and extracted her cigarette case from her bag, offering one across the table to Robin.

'Is it his money?' she asked abruptly.

Arrested, Robin raised her head to meet her look blankly. The ignored cigarette case lay open between them. Marina's lips twisted.

'The firm is doing well but we're not in the millionaire class. Have you decided to look after your future, Robin?'

Robin shook her head in disbelief. As she had said, Marina had known her for years. How could she suggest such a thing?

'I don't understand you,' she said, hurt.

Marina shrugged. 'Well, I must say I never thought you were mercenary. But when a woman gets to a certain age—especially a woman without a family to fall back on . . .'

Robin winced but said steadily, 'Believe me, it has nothing to do with his money.'

Marina extracted a cigarette and lit it, snapping the case shut with unnecessary force. 'So what *has* it to do with?'

Robin murmured, 'That's surely our affair?'

Marina blew out a long blue spiral of smoke before answering.

'I've known Guy a long time,' she said at last, surprising Robin. 'He doesn't wear his heart on his sleeve but, for all that, he feels things deeply.' She looked across the table with a needle sharp glance and then said deliberately, 'I haven't seen him as unhappy as he is now, since his father died.'

Robin gasped, whitening. 'And you think that's my fault?'

Marina's eyes narrowed. 'It seems a reasonable conclusion. You get engaged to him. You see as little of him as possible.' She ticked it off on her fingers. 'You never ring him, they tell me. You spend all your time at work. And what time you don't spend in the office goes

on design, as far as I can see.' She leaned forward. 'My
dear girl, you've done nine months' work in three weeks.
It's not natural.'

A small bitter smile that she could not control
flickered at the corner of Robin's mouth. 'Unconventional rather than unnatural,' she protested. 'And it's
not a conventional engagement, Marina. As Guy would
tell you if you were to ask him.'

'You mean you are not madly in love with each
other?' asked Marina sounding unsurprised.

Robin shivered. Ah, but she was in love. So deeply in
love she could not bear to think about it. But it was not
something to admit. 'No,' she said steadily.

Marina's gaze was unwavering and unusually
penetrating. 'You're sure?'

Robin thought of his laughter, the firm irresistible
touch and the blank unconcern he had shown about
seeing her. He wanted to marry her; she did not doubt
that. He made an excellent case for it. But, though she
was fairly sure she did not know all the reasons that he
wanted it, she knew that the most pressing was to
provide a chaperon for Laurel. And after that—well,
they were physically compatible as he had demonstrated.
Nor had she clung, as Dilly Cavanagh had clung; he
must reason that she would not weary him in that way.

Her eyes darkened. 'Quite sure,' she said with
unmistakable conviction.

Marina sighed. 'That's a pity,' she said unexpectedly.
'And makes it all the more extraordinary. Why did it
happen?'

'What?' said Robin, not really attending and then,
realising what she had said, how much she had given
away, went very still.

Marina's eyebrows flew up in undisguised astonishment. Trying and failing to put a brave face on it,
Robin's eyes fell before that expression.

'Oh *damn*!' she said in real distress, her hands pressing against her cheeks in a gesture of pure guilty instinct.

'I—see,' said Marina at last, slowly. She put the cigarette to her lips. 'You fell into bed with him—for the first time in your life, I imagine. And then blackmailed him with your innocence.'

'No,' cried Robin passionately. 'No. I didn't want . . .' She stopped herself then but too late.

'Didn't want to marry him,' concluded Marina coolly. She did not sound particularly surprised.

'I didn't say that,' Robin murmured.

'My dear girl, you didn't have to.' Marina stubbed her cigarette out with great deliberation and then looked up across the table at her very straightly. 'I suppose he's being quixotic. That would be like Guy. He always pays his debts. But he's making a grave mistake this time. And so are you.'

Not wanting to know what she meant but driven by something beyond herself, Robin asked, 'Why do you say that?'

'Because there is no substitute for love, my dear,' Marina said gravely. 'And you'll both find that out if you go with this madness.'

Robin could have answered that. Had she not already found out the truth of it? But even as she opened her lips to reply the waiter appeared with their food and she subsided, unregretful. Marina was unpredictable but Robin had little doubt that this time she meant well. Nevertheless, it was a subject that could only be discussed with Guy. If she could not talk it over with him, she could not confide in anyone. On the whole it was better to steer Marina away from any further comments on the present situation of her junior partner.

Marina herself made no further attempt to resurrect

the former topic of conversation and they had a
relatively pleasant lunch discussing clients and the state
of the business. The only slight embarrassment occurred
when Marina asked after the state of the Gerrard house
in Hill Place. As Robin was able to tell her that it was
virtually finished and awaited only the arrival of the
furniture which she was going to oversee herself over
the next few days, that, too, passed off without remark.

There was a message from Guy's secretary when they
got back to the office: would Robin telephone.
Marina's eyebrows rose to her hairline.

'You talk to his *secretary*?'

'He's very busy,' Robin murmured excusingly,
dialling on the line Sally had given her, half turning her
back on her companions.

Sally and Marina exchanged meaning glances as she
did so.

'Miss Lambert? Robin Dale here. I got your
message.'

'Oh yes, Miss Dale. Thank you for calling back.'
Guy's secretary had a frosty voice which made no
concessions to friendliness to her employer's fiancée.
'Mr Gerrard asked whether you would meet him at the
house this evening. At' she paused, obviously consulting
a desk diary, 'seven o'clock. He has a meeting but he
should be through by then. And if he isn't, you have a
key, haven't you?'

'Yes,' agreed Robin. '*We*,' she stressed the pronoun
ever so slightly, 'have a key. Tell Mr Gerrard I will be
there.'

She was, though it was some time after seven that she
arrived. She told herself that she had been delayed
unavoidably by last-minute tasks that had taken longer
than she expected. The truth, however, was that she had
spun out her tasks to make sure that she did not leave
the office on time. She quite passionately did not want

to sit alone in his empty house waiting for him. It slightly chilled her to reflect that the empty house might be one that she would share with him; almost certainly would be.

She let herself in with the security key suspended from the distinctive key-ring that bore the logo of Marina Interiors. The house was silent.

She raised her voice tentatively, calling 'Guy?'

He emerged from the drawing room at once. She thought at first that he looked rather grim, but it had to be a trick of the evening sunshine because when she came close up to him she saw he was smiling down at her with his habitual lazy amusement. He dropped a light kiss on her brow.

'Hello, lover. You're late.'

'I know. I'm sorry. I got held up,' Robin muttered.

Guy grinned. 'Up to now, that's always been *my* line on dates. You're a very salutary experience, Robin Dale.'

She laughed, trying to make it sound natural. 'Because I keep you waiting? But I thought that was the woman's prerogative.'

'No.' For a moment the hint of harshness returned but he pinched her chin and chuckled and the bitter lines disappeared. 'It's the prerogative of the one who has least to lose. You knew that if you stood me up I'd come and fetch you. Didn't you?'

'No,' she said indignantly, adding with a touch of mischief, 'If I had, I'd have waited and got a lift down here in your beautiful car. Instead of which I walked and my legs ache as a result.'

'Idle female,' he teased, taking her hand and tucking it through his arm.

At his touch, as always, Robin felt something begin to melt and move inside her. Instinctively she stiffened against that unwilling attraction. Guy must have felt it because, momentarily, his fingers tightened. But when she did not try to withdraw her hand he relaxed again, taking her into the drawing room without a word.

'Did you want to talk about furniture?' Robin asked with an effort. 'It's all coming this week, you know. You can move in as soon as you like next week.'

He looked down at her, his lashes hiding his expression from her. 'And how soon do you want to move in?'

'Me?' It was a squeak. Robin took a steadying breath and managed, 'I didn't know we were talking about me.'

'Didn't you?' His mouth curved in what might have been irony. 'And where did you expect I would want my wife to live? In an apartment block with a twenty-four hour porter to protect her from me?'

Robin moved her hand and stepped away from him. 'Not at all,' she said coolly. 'When I am your wife, I will of course live wherever you choose. But the date is still some time away.'

Guy looked at her for a long moment, his expression unreadable, his body oddly taut. Then he took a piece of paper from his pocket and almost flung it down on the window seat. It fluttered and fell to the floor. Robin looked at him enquiringly and then, disturbed by something she could not put a name to, bent and retrieved it.

It was a marriage licence. She stared at it disbelievingly.

'When——' she began, her voice cracking with strain.

'Three days,' he told her, answering the half-enunciated question.

She swallowed nervously, not knowing what to say. The flimsy sheet of official paper shook in her fingers. She turned it over, smoothing it out with a trembling hand.

'I thought Friday. They can fit us in at eleven. I assumed you would not want a church wedding.'

Robin looked down at the form. 'I—I never really thought about it,' she said with hesitant honesty.

His mouth moved in the vestige of a smile. 'That is patently obvious. I said you were unusual, didn't I? My stepmother lives in the firm belief that all girls spend their time between leaving primary school and getting married in planning the wedding ceremony. She will not believe in your indifference.' He paused and his voice lost its wryness and became bleak. 'But I do.'

Robin was fiddling with the paper in her hand, rolling it absorbedly into a screw from one corner. She felt somehow that she owed him an apology for her deficiency in this respect.

'It's because I never expected to get married,' she offered in a thin voice. 'I suppose.'

Guy nodded coolly, his face unreadable. 'I dare say that would be it.'

Robin licked dry lips. 'And—after Friday—do you want to move in here?' she asked huskily. 'I mean, do you want me to move in as well?'

His eyelids lifted briefly and she flinched from what she saw there. Then he smiled quite pleasantly and she wondered if she had been mistaken in the wild rage she had thought she detected.

'That would be the best, I think,' he affirmed. 'Laurel will come with us, of course. She will be able to help you get the place straight. It will do her good. I shall not be able to do much, myself, I'm afraid. I have rather a heavy schedule just at present. Though I am intending to take some time off later and take you away for a real honeymoon.'

Robin whitened at the thought.

'And, of course,' he added softly, watching her, 'I will be here in the evenings.'

She swallowed. 'Of—of course.'

Guy turned away, then, as if he had lost interest once her capitulation was assured.

'That's settled then,' he said calmly. 'I've told my kind landlady that I'm moving out. It suits her very well because she will be back in London herself tomorrow. And Laurel is looking forward to changing her abode.'

'Yes, I'm sure she is,' said Robin in a faint voice, trying to adjust to this new shock.

Take it calmly, she told herself. You knew it was coming. Take it steadily and it will be all right. He is not a monster and you are not a child. As long as you do not panic and throw a scene, there is nothing to worry about. Hundreds of people marry every day, a good many of them with less good will and respect than you have. Just hold on and stay *calm*.

'Rose wants us to go to drinks with her tonight,' he went on in a casual voice. 'She's got a few people coming. I said we'd look in.' He paused. 'So you'd better have your evidence for them to gawp at.'

Robin stared at him, uncomprehending. Guy was shaken by a silent laugh.

'No, I don't suppose that had occurred to you, either, had it?'

She found he was holding out a small velvet-covered box to her. Slowly, almost reluctantly, she reached out a hand and he dropped it into her palm. She opened the box. She was staring at a magnificent pearl, set in diamonds and antique gold. It was plainly old. She wondered for a moment whether he had given her his mother's ring, the one Laurel had spoken of, but his next words disillusioned her.

'I chose it because I liked it, though they tell me pearls are unlucky. But it's more—frivolous—than anything I've seen you wear. I think you would be the better for a little more frivolity. And I am sure,' he added ironically, 'that you are not the sort of girl to be superstitious.'

Robin looked down at the beautiful thing, faintly chilled. Had he not given her his mother's ring because he did not expect this marriage to be permanent and did not want a family heirloom to go to a stranger?

She said in a constricted tone, 'Thank you. It's very beautiful.'

'Put it on.'

She fumbled with it. She seldom wore jewellery, hardly ever rings. It was not as heavy as it looked and she nearly dropped it in surprise. Guy made an impatient noise and took her left hand, holding it steady while he slid the ring on to her finger. It fitted perfectly.

'Laurel pinched one of your gloves,' he told her with a glimmer of humour. 'I told her to get a ring but she said she couldn't find one at your flat. I wanted it to fit right from the start but if the glove was misleading it will be easy enough to alter the size.'

Robin shook her head. 'No, it's fine.'

He squeezed her fingers. 'You say that now but wait until you've had it on twenty-four hours. You may feel differently then. Let me know if you do.'

'Yes, of course,' she said politely. 'Thank you.'

He gave her a quick look and then shrugged his shoulders. 'Don't thank me. Part of the necessary trappings. Now that you've got it, let us go to Rose's.'

Robin followed him out to the car, a faint worried crease between her brows. There had been the slightest hint of squaring his shoulders in that last remark, as if he was already regretting their bargain and its consequences. She bit her lip. She could not expect anything else. In his place she would be regretting it all, too.

She said hesitantly, 'Guy, there's no need—well, I mean—if you change your mind . . .'

He was helping her into the Mercedes. He looked down at her. 'I told you at Willow Grove,' he said harshly. 'I shan't change my mind. And neither will you.'

She stared up at him. For a horrifying moment she felt the tears rush to her eyes, and rapidly looked away, blinking. She thought she heard him swear under his breath and, in embarrassment at her loss of control, leaned forward and pulled the passenger door shut against her side.

In silence Guy stepped back and came round to the driver's seat, getting in and closing the door with more force than the operation seemed strictly to warrant. Robin stared straight ahead. Her hand felt weighed down by the ring he had placed on it. She touched it uncomfortably as he put the car into gear and they moved forward.

The journey was accomplished in unbroken silence. When they drew up outside a large, many-balconied block in Kensington, Robin looked at it in frozen surprise. She had never been here before.

'I told you that I moved out when Rose started entertaining Dilly Cavanagh,' Guy remarked, observing her reaction. 'Rose will be making her own arrangements now. Laurel will live with us and I shall get rid of this place.'

Robin could not suppress a little shiver at the intimate image his words inevitably conjured up. But she did her best to suppress it. Just as she let her hand lie heavily in his as they made their way up to the Gerrard apartment and went in through wide open double doors.

Guy had said that Rose was having a few people in for drinks but it looked to Robin's not unsophisticated eye like a full-scale party for a hundred people or more. There were waitresses in black dresses with spotless frilly white aprons, handing canapés round on silver trays. And white-coated waiters were offering champagne or a variety of spirits.

Taking a tall glass of champage from a passing tray, Guy presented it to her with a little grimace.

'I'm sorry. I didn't realise she was up to this sort of thing,' he said ruefully. 'Though I suppose I should have expected it. Rose seizes any excuse for a party.'

'I think it's very flattering,' said Robin composedly. 'And we'd better circulate. It's the least we can do.'

There was a gleam of admiration in his eyes. He nodded slowly. 'All right. We'll circulate for an hour. Then we go.'

She gave him a shy smile. 'I'd like that.'

'Robin——' he said impulsively in a low voice, 'Robin I——'

But they were interrupted. And by the time she had been introduced to the interruptor and received his congratulations the party had eddied round them and there was no opportunity for quiet conversation between them.

Rose Gerrard, slightly to Robin's surprise, was perfectly friendly in a rather vague way. She was a pretty, faded woman with a fluffy manner that Robin suspected was quite carefully cultivated. But she was polite, thanking Robin for taking Laurel into her new home and deprecating her daughter's historic exploits.

'You will be such an excellent *example*,' she murmured. 'Being a *working* girl. So original of Guy!'

It left Robin feeling like a piece of utilitarian furniture imported as an experiment into a gracious salon. She was, however, shrewd enough to suspect that it was done deliberately and even to be slightly amused by it.

She was not amused, though, when she came face to face with Lady Cavanagh to be greeted by much more open and unashamed malice.

'Well, well, Cinderella in person,' said Lady Cavanagh spitefully, not attempting to lower her voice. 'How does it feel to get to go to the ball at last, darling?'

Robin was startled. She did not think Dilly Cavanagh was her friend but this display of open resentment hurt nobody but Lady Cavanagh herself. She suspected that the woman had had too much to drink.

Several heads had turned at the loud remark. Across the room Robin saw Guy's expression as he began to shoulder his way purposefully through the crowd towards them. She felt sorry for Dilly.

'Do you turn back to your rags at midnight?' she was saying insultingly. 'Or has Guy made sure that you dress respectably?'

'I don't think I'm a very likely Cinderella, Lady Cavanagh,' Robin said as gently as she could.

The ravaged face so close to her own stared for a moment and then contorted with hysterical laughter.

'Maybe not. Maybe you're right there. More like Lolita.'

Robin stiffened like a tautened bowstring. It could just be chance, of course. It could be sheer ill luck that Dilly Cavanagh had struck on the name that some of the gutter press had attached to her ten years ago. But there was something horribly knowing in the woman's glittering glance.

She said crisply, 'I don't know what you're talking about.'

Dilly Cavanagh waved a thin hand before her face. After a moment Robin realised that she was wagging a finger at her accusingly. She was so drunk, though, that the gesture was unrecognisable. A sick disgust took hold of Robin. It must have shown in her face.

'Don't you look down your nose at me, you bitch,'

the enemy hissed. 'I know all about you. Shushu,' she had trouble with the name, hiccuped and tried again, 'Shushu told me and I looked you up. It's all in my files back at the paper.'

Robin felt a terrifying faintness well up. This was worse than she had ever imagined could happen, though she had lain awake at nights in a cold sweat fearing that her stepfather would find her. But that was years ago and she had allowed herself to forget.

From behind her Guy had arrived. He put a firm hand on her shoulder. It felt as heavy as an iron bar and as inescapable.

Dilly said with blurred satisfaction, 'Did you know that your intended was a long-time seducer of susceptible older men, darling? Have you hit premature middle age?'

The weight on Robin's shoulder became savage. She felt as if she were being ground down into the floor by it.

He said, 'You're drunk, Dilly,' on a tolerant, friendly voice, utterly at variance with that ferocious grip. 'You'd better lie down and have a pint or two of black coffee.'

She gave an hysterical laugh that broke. 'Oh no, darling, it's not the drink talking. I can prove it.' She leant towards him in a hideous parody of confiding and said in a loud whisper, 'Shall I show you my scrapbook?'

Guy's hand dropped from Robin and took Dilly's elbow as she swayed. 'Yes, of course,' he said, kindly, soothingly. 'Whatever you like. Come with me and we'll find you that coffee.'

She clung to him giggling, 'And somewhere to lie down, too, like you said.'

'That, too.' He looked at Robin across Dilly's head. 'Will you tell the staff to bring that coffee into the

chintz room please, Robin. Or better still, bring it
yourself.'

He steeered Dilly away through the crowd without a
backward look. Numbly, Robin did as she was told. A
great dread was beginning to build up inside her. He
had looked—remote. He had told her that he would not
forgive it if she withheld the truth. And she had done.
She could not bear to do anything else.

Now, it seemed all too likely that drunken Dilly
would spill out the old sordid story for him to hear
without any of the explanations that she, Robin, could
make in extenuation. Oh, if only she had been braver. If
only she had told him the whole truth when he asked.

Perhaps he would not believe Dilly. She was not in a
state to be believed, with her intoxicated gestures and
slurred speech. Perhaps he would put it down to the
unsubstantiated malice of a rejected and uncontrolled
woman.

Robin collected the coffee and went along to the
room that the waitress had absently indicated to her.
She knew that it was a vain hope. Dilly had been too
triumphant. She had mentioned her scrapbook, too;
presumably she had unearthed the old press reports.
Robin could remember them, even after all these years.
They had seared her to the bone when she eighteen.
There were phrases she had never succeeded in
forgetting.

She pushed open the door and went into the chintz
room; it took all the courage at her command.

The first thing she saw was the couch was empty,
Lady Cavanagh, if she was lying down, was not doing it
in this pleasant sitting room. The room was empty
except for Guy. He was standing by the open window,
looking down at something in his hand. Robin paused.
Just in that first second her brain refused to accept the
evidence of her own eyes. It was too cruel. It could not

happen. Even Dilly Cavanagh would not do this to a fellow creature.

Then hearing the door, he turned. And she realised that it was true. He was standing there reading a little sheaf of yellowed press cuttings. Robin did not need to be told what they contained.

She made a little sound of distress. Guy looked at her coolly.

'You'd better put the coffee down, Miranda. Before you spill it.' She froze with pain at his light, sarcastic tone. 'That is right, isn't it? Miranda Jane Tyrell-Brown. White hope of the British stage until she seduced her mother's husband and disappeared?'

Robin put the cup down carefully on a satinwood table, her gestures mechanical. There was a small mat on another table and she placed it tenderly under the saucer. Some of the coffee slopped into the saucer. She observed it distantly. Her hand must be shaking more than she had realised. She was not normally so clumsy.

She straightened, her eyes perfectly blank.

'Yes, that's right,' she said in a calm voice, drained of emotion.

He flung the sheaf of cuttings aside and took an impatient stride towards her.

'Why didn't you tell me? *Why*?'

'I did,' she reminded him. 'All the facts.'

'But not what happened afterwards. Not about how they put out pleas for you, sent detectives after you, filled the papers with all that,' a contemptuous gesture at the cuttings, 'stuff.'

Robin said sadly, 'Would it have made any difference?'

His eyes were furious. 'Of course it would have made a bloody difference. What the hell do you think I am?'

He meant she was not a fit person to take charge of his sister, Robin thought painfully. The intervening years, her career and her present character, were as nothing compared with a ten-year-old scandal. She retreated.

He said, 'Felix knows, doesn't he?'

She said, 'Of course. I ran away to him ...' and realised too late how it sounded.

Guy swore. His face was white with those fearsome indentations like sword slashes down his cheeks. His right hand clenched tight.

'Tell me, Robin,' his voice was mild but Robin was not deceived, 'why did you bother to see me at all?'

She stared, uncomprehending.

'Marina was right, wasn't she?' he said giving way to savagery. 'She told me it was for revenge. But she thought it was something to do with the little girl out of finishing school who used to make sheep's eyes at me. Only it wasn't. It was part of your great revenge on all mankind.' He stopped, breathing angrily, before adding in a voice as soft as silk, 'Or rather, all mankind except Felix Lamont.'

She said rapidly, 'Felix was a friend of my father's, my real father. He helped me, that's all. He put me up, when I ran away. Helped me find a job. He talked to my mother for me. He told her I was safe but I wasn't coming back.'

Guy's eyes narrowed. 'Your mother *knew* you were safe? And yet she let that circus go on?'

Robin shuddered. 'Francis—my stepfather—wouldn't accept that I wasn't coming back. My mother couldn't control him. Nobody could. He did what he wanted and be damned to the consequences—to himself or anybody else.'

'Are you sure that he wasn't suspicious of the interest Felix showed in you?'

She shrugged. 'Possibly. He was suspicious of everything.'

Guy said deliberately, 'If he was in love with an icy little bitch like you, I'm not surprised.'

She gasped, whitening.

He smiled slowly, almost cruelly. 'Does that frighten you, Robin? I don't see why it should. After all, you've always known that your stepfather and I were two of a kind, haven't you? You more or less told me as much.'

She said on a note of pleading, 'Guy—put yourself in my place—I learned to be wary of men like that.'

'Oh you did. You did indeed. And to go for them with all the weapons in your armoury whenever you identified one of us.'

'*No!* It wasn't like that . . .'

She was giving herself away with every word, every gesture. It was only a short step to telling him of her love for him. And that would be a real disaster because that would put her finally in his power.

'Was?' Guy said again, not taking his eyes from her face. 'You mean you think this ends it?'

She said, 'Surely . . .'

'You are wrong, lover,' he told her with deadly intent. 'It doesn't make the slightest difference to—this.'

His hands took her by the shoulders and pulled her inexorably against his body. His heart was racing. Robin stumbled, falling against him off balance and incapable of levering herself away. She looked up at him, filled with despair.

The magnificent eyes glinted like chips of sapphire ice. She had never seen him, or imagined seeing him, so coldly angry. All the friendliness, all the beguiling laughter, was wiped away as if it had never been. This, then, was the man underneath the mask, the man she had sensed uneasily on earlier occasions. And this was what really lay between them—this searing attraction more like enmity than love.

Robin gave a half sob and tried to pull away.

'No,' he said. 'No, not this time, lover.'

'Let me go,' she said between stiff lips.

Guy's laugh was insolent, without amusement.

'Why should I? What have I got to lose? You already know everything there is to know about me. I'm like your stepfather, aren't I? Wicked. Brutal. Uncontrollable. You know it all. So I needn't pretend any more, need I?'

His kiss was savage. There was no love there, no kindness. But even in his bitter rage he still desired her and took no trouble to disguise the fact. Half stifled, Robin gave a protesting moan which was cut off by his hard mouth.

At first she fought him, full of horror and self-disgust. But she was no match for him when he chose to exert his full strength against her. He overcame her resistance easily; and not just her resistance but her shrinking distaste. In the end it was not just a matter of his superior strength. He forced her not to submit to him, as Francis would have done, but to admit the surging hunger in her own blood.

When she fell back on to the cushioned couch she was trembling, but not with fear. As the fierce body imposed itself on her she reached for him, welcoming the ruthless passion and responding with abandon.

For countless whirling moments she was lost, driven to the peak of necessity and driving as she was driven. When release came she was weeping with need, clinging to his shoulders like a desperate clawing cat.

After a while he detached her arms and stood up. Robin lay half dazed, watching him as he straightened his clothes. The white shirt was open and half off. He shrugged his shoulders back into the cloth and began to button it. His hand was perfectly steady as he did so.

Humiliated, Robin turned her head away. Hot tears began to seep uncontrollably down her face. Her lashes were sticky with them. She did not brush them away but let them fall silently.

Guy said coolly, 'There's no point in crying. I have proved my point, I believe.'

Robin struggled with her voice. It did not sound like her own when it came, so husky was it with weariness and defeat.

'Yes. You've done that.'

'And I suppose you hate me for it. But, by your own account you can't have expected anything else. Not from men like me which you know so well.'

She raised herself carefully, adjusting her dress as she did so.

'No, I suppose not. Marina was saying only this afternoon that you pay your debts.'

He skimmed a look over her in her dishevelment, seeing the distress she was so desperately trying to disguise. His mouth twisted. Seeing that fleeting expression Robin averted her eyes, swinging herself to her feet so that she was, at least, on a level with him and meeting his accusations squarely.

Guy said, 'Marina was saying? Ah, that's the trouble, isn't it, lover? It matters more what the Marinas of this world—and the Laurels and the Dilly Cavanaghs—say, than what I tell you.' He ran his hand through his hair. 'If only you'd listened to me instead of the gossips . . .'

Robin was looking down at her ring. 'I did listen to you,' she said in a remote little voice. 'While you made your plans and gave your instructions. And issued your threats.' The golden eyes lifted for a brief moment and regarded him without expression. 'You said that if I tried to keep anything from you, you would make me sorry that I ever met you. Well, I did.' She looked down at the ring again. 'And you have.'

'Robin——' he began in an urgent voice, but she was not listening.

She took the ring off her finger, twisting it this way and that to ease it. Then she put it down gently beside the now cold coffee before looking up at him for one last, painful, time.

'You made your point Guy. I hope—now—I've made mine.'

He said nothing, standing like a statue as she turned her back on him and walked silently out of the room.

CHAPTER ELEVEN

'ROBIN? Are you there?'

Robin started, coming out of her daydream with a jump. Her sketch pad slid from her knees. She was picking it up as Alice Jones came round the corner.

'So, this is where you are,' she said, smiling. She was carrying a pretty tray set with a couple of steaming mugs and a plate of biscuits. 'Geoff said he thought you'd gone out but Mum said you were in the garden.'

Robin stood up and took the tray from her, smiling wryly at its burden. Ever since she had arrived on the Jones' doorstep three weeks ago, Alice and her mother-in-law had conceived a single minded plan to make Robin consume as much of their home cooking as would bring her back to what they regarded as a healthy weight. Robin, with her appetite completely lost, had proved a disappointment, but they were persistent. The biscuits on the tray were clearly hot from the oven.

Alice sank down on to the grass beside Robin's deck chair and took her coffee. 'Were you asleep?'

Robin shook her head, indicating her sketch pad. 'Trying, not very successfully, to work.'

Alice nodded with understanding. When she was unhappy she went through the house with her sponges and flannels and polishing rags. She knew all about hard work as therapy. Of course, Robin Dale's work was more specialised and certainly better paid than her own. But that did not make much of a difference to the spirit in which it was done.

'Any luck?'

Robin shrugged. 'A little. The trouble is I'm working from memory. I really ought to go back to the office to collect the file. That has all the necessary details in it. But I—can't.'

Alice was thoughtful.

'You'll have to go back to the office some time,' she observed into her coffee. 'Won't you? It's not as if you're just an employee and can walk out whenever you feel like it. You're a director. You've got responsibilities.'

Robin bit her lip.

'Isn't that so?' said Alice with gentle persistence.

'Yes. You're right, of course. And anyway I can't stay here for ever. I shall have to go back to my flat. I can't impose on you and Geoff for much longer.'

Alice turned a genuinely startled face towards her. 'There's no question of imposition. We love having you. And you give Geoff ideas,' she added mischievously. 'You're obviously an inspiration to him. In his work that is.'

Robin smiled. 'Still . . .'

'Still, you can't run away for ever.'

'No.' Robin's lashes flickered and the heavy brows drew together as if in pain, Alice noted with concern. 'No, I shall have to go back and face him—them—some time.'

Wisely, Alice said nothing. She had seen the notice of Geoff's best customer's engagement to Guy Gerrard and been suitably thrilled. When that same customer had turned up with Geoff in the car one evening, all but distraught, having fled to Geoff's workroom, Alice had been too kind and too clever to ask questions. They had offered the desperate girl sanctuary, told Marina where she was staying, asked no questions and waited until she chose to confide.

So far she had said nothing but that she had had a

disagreement with her fiancé. She was, observed Alice, wearing no ring either.

Daily Robin scanned the papers, all the papers. They could only guess what it was that she was looking for. Daily she had sat back afterwards with a sigh, discarding them at once after that preliminary anxious investigation.

Now Alice sat in silent sympathy and sipped her coffee.

At length Robin said, 'Perhaps I could—tomorrow when he—when they are all at work. I could go back to my flat then.'

'And afterwards?'

Robin shrugged. 'I don't know. Go abroad, perhaps. I've had offers to work in New York.'

'Will that solve the problem?' asked Alice, pretty certain that the problem was over six foot, blue-eyed and commuted to New York on a fairly regular basis.

Robin shivered in spite of the heat of the sun. 'I—can't be sure. Perhaps not. But I can't face,' she hesitated, 'I can't face London any longer. I know that.'

Alice shrugged. 'If you say so.' She lifted her head. 'That's the doorbell. I'd better go. Geoff is down at the warehouse and Mum is washing her hair. She'll never hear it.'

She rose gracefully and left to answer the door. Alone, Robin stared unseeingly into the cold coffee she did not want. Alice was right, of course. If she ran away again she would only take her pain with her. The only real solution was to turn and fight; to see Guy, if necessary; to carry on her career as if nothing had happened. After all she was not the first woman to be crossed in love. She ought to have more backbone than to let it destroy her whole life.

But just the thought of seeing Guy again, however remotely, however casually, was enough to set her thoughts off on to a trail of panic. If he was still angry, what might he do to her? What might he say? And if he was not angry, if he had dismissed the whole matter and was now completely indifferent, how much worse would that be?

She dropped her head in her hands. Every day she had searched the papers for some notice that their engagement was cancelled. She had not found it. The gossip columns, though she cared less about them, were equally silent. You would have thought there had never been a tycoon called Guy Gerrard in whose every move their readers—or at least their editors—were avidly interested.

A voice she knew said wryly above her head, 'Praying, lover?'

Her hands dropped and she raised her eyes in absolute disbelief. He was here, *here*. He was just the same, looking at her with vivid amusement, tall and powerful and utterly at his ease.

She said, 'You,' in a whisper.

His mouth twisted. 'Me. Are you going to scream?'

He flung himself down on the grass, stretching his long legs out in front of him, and leaning back on his elbow to offer his face to the sun.

Robin took hold of herself. She was an adult, not a child. And anyway this man had already done his worst.

She said coolly, 'Do you think I should?'

Guy gave her a long ironic look, 'On past form, I wouldn't blame you if you did.'

She inclined her head. 'Quite.'

'This time, however, all I want is to talk. I promise not to lay a hand on you if it helps.' Bitterness invaded his voice. 'If you can believe me.'

Robin was aware of an odd compunction. 'I will trust you.'

'That's—very generous of you.'

He was silent, seemingly at a loss.

She prompted, 'Talk about what?'

Guy said, 'My former landlady is back in town.'

Robin was nonplussed. 'So?' she asked in bewilderment.

'So she's been telling me about the Tyrell company and, in particular, your stepfather.'

Robin flinched. 'I see.'

'You were wrong in thinking people did not know how he was hounding you,' he said in a conversational tone. 'Sue told me all about it. A girlfriend of hers was in the company, apparently. They were all very indignant, I gather. But of course he was their employer so they couldn't do anything.' He paused. 'Sue tells me nobody who knew anything about it believed the story the papers printed about you being a predatory Lolita figure.'

Robin swallowed. 'I see,' she said again. She looked away. 'And now you also know something about it, I suppose you don't believe the story either?'

'Lover, I didn't believe it anyway,' he told her in a flat voice.

She shot him an incredulous look. 'That—was not the impression you gave me.'

He said, 'I was hurt, shaken, angry—and jealous.'

'*Jealous?*' She did not believe her ears.

'Look——' He sat up and half reached for her hand before thinking better of it and placing both his, palms down, on the grass. He frowned. 'I knew there was something else, something you weren't telling me. When you admitted that Felix knew—which I'd always suspected anyway—I went up like a volcano. It wasn't till afterwards that I realised you were saying that he was a sort of honorary uncle. All I could think of was that you loved and trusted him.

And you wouldn't love and trust me in a month of Sundays.'

She said with difficulty, 'I didn't trust anyone. Not even Felix.'

'No. I know that now, too.'

She stared.

'I've been to see him,' Guy told her wryly. 'We had a long talk. In which I discovered that I knew a good deal more about you than he did.'

Robin gave him a painful smile. 'You threatened once to have me investigated. Did you do so in the end?'

Guy looked really shocked. 'Of course not. How can you think it?'

She shrugged. 'Well, you wanted to know whether I was fit to take charge of Laurel or not. And, as you eventually established, I am not.'

He shut his eyes briefly. 'Oh God, the way my tactics have backfired ...' He opened his eyes and this time took both her hands very firmly. 'Listen, my darling, Laurel was a stratagem. I wanted to marry you, fast, before you had time to think or got away, and Laurel was the best excuse I could think of.'

'But—but it was because of Laurel that you postponed your Polish trip,' stammered Robin, her hands twitching in his grasp. 'And that you came back early.'

Guy shook her hands fiercely. 'Of course it wasn't,' he said in exasperation and when she stared at him went on, 'Oh God, I told you that you didn't know who was in love with you, didn't I? Don't you realise that I have been desperately in love ever since I set eyes on you?'

Robin shook her head.

'Laurel's a nice kid and I'm fond of her,' Guy allowed, 'but I don't cut short important business trips because she's fed up with doing the rounds of the shops with her mother and decamps with her boyfriend. It was because of *you*, because I had to set my stamp on you, because I knew you were the only woman in the world for me and everybody kept telling me that I hadn't a chance with you. Laurel was just camouflage.'

Robin said blankly, 'But you didn't care about me. Not a damn. You said,' it was a painful memory, 'that you had nothing to lose with me.'

Guy groaned. 'You have the most appalling ability to take things the wrong way. If I ever said that, what I meant was that, as your opinion of me was rock bottom anyway. I couldn't drive it any lower by any action of mine.'

'I don't believe it.'

'Don't you?' His mouth moved wryly. 'Do you remember once saying to me that you would fight fire with fire? Well, you did. I couldn't get close. Every meeting was a sort of battle. We were like enemies from the start. I knew you feared and perhaps disliked me. It made no difference.'

Robin shivered, recalling suddenly how she had felt that first evening, that first night in his arms; as if he was long familiar and she had come home.

'I know,' she said in a low voice.

The azure eyes lifted, became brilliant.

'*Do* you? I wondered . . .'

'I felt that no matter how strange—and, and wrong—it felt, that somehow it was almost inevitable. It frightened me.'

Guy raised her hands between both his and stroked his cheek across them.

'Odd. That's what reassured me.'

She stared at him helplessly. 'I don't understand you.'

'No?' He sounded wry. 'Well, I can't blame you. I haven't been behaving exactly rationally. What I am trying to say is that I want to marry you.'

Robin eased her hands out of his. There was a long silence while she considered his announcement. Her brow creased. Was this another instance of the quixotic Guy Gerrard doing the honourable thing? Marina had said he always paid his debts and Robin believed it.

She said with difficulty, 'Guy just because I—you—because it was the first time for me, that doesn't make me your responsibility, you know. It was my decision as much as yours. I wanted it, too.'

Disconcertingly, his eyes danced. 'I'm glad to hear you say that. The other possibility has, I must confess, given me one or two bad moments.'

'Other possibility?'

'That I really was the wicked seducer. That you were unwilling.'

Robin shook her head firmly. 'No.'

'No?' Guy stretched again, a lithe languorous animal in the sun. But he was watching her carefully, she knew.

'*No*. You have no need to feel guilty.' She gave him a false smile. 'So the offer of honourable matrimony is quite unnecessary.'

Guy moved closer though he did not touch her. His face became oddly serious. 'It was very necessary. And you're not listening, lover. I didn't offer anything. I made a statement. I want to marry you. It is perfectly simple.'

The hollow smile died on her face leaving her staring at him in bewilderment. '*Want* to . . .?'

'You don't have much of an opinion of either of us, do you?' Guy said in a resigned tone. 'Is it so very surprising?'

'But I'm not—well, beautiful. Or—or homelike. I have no training at being part of a family. I could only make you uncomfortable,' stammered Robin stampeded into total frankness by the unexpectedness of it.

There was a pause.

Then, 'You make me come alive,' said Guy abruptly.

She stared down at him, lost for words, despair warring with faint, burgeoning hope. He slewed round and reached up a hand to cradle her cheek in a soft, tentative caress.

'Think about it, my darling. Whatever I may be—whatever you have heard about me—I'm not the sort of man that makes love to prickly ladies the first time he has dinner with them. But with you—it was instantaneous. You were so special, so important, that I dared not even wait to get past the prickles. I had to have my stamp on you fast before you got away and decided you didn't need me to stir up your life for you.'

Robin sat very still, hardly daring to breathe. Guy sighed and his hand fell away.

'And that was the start of the trouble, wasn't it? You didn't like men with too much worldly success under their belt anyway. They reminded you of your stepfather. And then, by snatching what I wanted like that, I only succeeded in convincing you that I was out of the same mould.'

Robin said in a strangled voice, 'I *told* you. It was mutual. You didn't snatch any more than I did.'

Guy looked at her doubtfully. 'No? Then why did everything go so wrong? I thought it was because you couldn't forgive me for rushing you like that.'

Robin shook her head. The brilliant eyes narrowed.

'Then what in the name of God was it?'

'Me,' whispered Robin. 'It was me. I was—I am too afraid. I—can't compete.'

He shook his head in disbelief. 'Compete with what? With whom? What are you talking about?'

'The others,' she said miserably. 'The women who love you. The ones who would be suitable wives. The ones who are discarded mistresses.' She made a wide, despairing gesture. 'The whole species.'

Guy said incredulously, 'You think you're in some sort of race and you're going to lose?' He sat up very straight and turned her face so that she could not avoid his penetrating gaze. 'Where did you get that idea?'

Her lips moved in a travesty of a smile. 'I've always known that I wasn't marriageable, if that's what you mean.'

He dismissed that with a contemptuous, impatient hand. 'Nobody is marriageable. At least not until they meet the person that they can't live without marrying. No, this nonsense about competitors. Did it seem to you that you had any rivals? When I spent all my spare time—and some that wasn't spare,' he added with self-mockery, 'with you?'

Robin bit her lip. 'No. But Laurel told me about Lady Cavanagh.'

If anything his bewilderment seemed to deepen. 'What has that stupid bitch got to do with it?'

Robin blushed. His eyes widened.

'You mean you thought I was having a fling with Dilly Cavanagh?' he said, barely above a breath. 'Laurel told you so?'

She nodded.

'Oh, dear God.' Guy almost flung himself away from her. 'Look.' He was making an effort to keep calm, she could see, though his fingers flexed as if he would like to do someone a mischief if they came with strangling distance. 'Dilly Cavanagh married an old friend of mine. When she got through most of his money she dumped him. He was relieved. I didn't give a damn. But she struck up some sort of a friendship with my stepmother. Rose,' he said dispassionately, 'is one of the silliest women I know. And she likes company, lots of it. She particularly likes other women to go on long shopping binges with. Laurel, as you can imagine, has not been willing to oblige. Dilly Cavanagh has filled the bill.'

He glanced round the garden, as if looking for sanity.

'She was always inviting Dilly to places. She invites lots of people, including me sometimes. The papers started to say we were "very-good-friends" but then Dilly's a columnist and well placed to drop the right hints. I don't read those sort of papers so I didn't know. Laurel does.'

Robin said, 'But there had to be something in it. She was so desperate. That day she came to my flat, as well as that last evening.'

She shuddered, remembering. He reached up and took her hand firmly but with great tenderness. She stilled.

'Yes, there was something in it. In her mind, poor woman. You must have realised she is not—entirely—in command of herself. She has a drinking problem. Even Rose has now noticed it. She needs help.'

Torn with pity, Robin said, 'Oh poor creature. How dreadful.'

'You can say that after what she handed out to you?' Guy asked in patent disbelief.

'But she will have to live with that for the rest of her life. Even when she's cured she will have to live with that humiliation. Besides,' Robin lowered her eyes to their clasped hands, 'it is terrible to be so much in love.'

His hand tightened. He moved so that he was kneeling on the grass in front of her, the azure eyes shining and very intent.

'Is it?'

'I—I imagine so.'

'Robin, look at me.'

Slowly, warily, she raised her eyes to his.

'Robin, my darling, my lover: I love you desperately. I can't tell you how much. I tried but I'm no good at that sort of thing and I was so afraid——'

'*Afraid?*'

His expression was ironic. 'One look and I collapsed in a heap at your feet. But it didn't seem mutual. It seemed to me then that I couldn't get near you. So I resorted to shock tactics and you wrote me off as a bully like your stepfather.'

'No!' Robin protested.

'Oh yes you did, lover. Don't try to be kind to me. If you hadn't been afraid of me, why didn't you tell me about what happened ten years ago? Above all, why did you run away from me?'

'But I did tell you.' She sat up in agitation. 'Don't you understand? I told you more than I've ever told anyone else in my life. I couldn't bear to think about it. As for not naming names,' she shrugged. 'I would have done in time, I suspect. But I'd already made such a revolutionary step forward I wasn't ready to go any further. Can you understand that?'

A sad smile touched the fine mouth. 'Oh yes,' he said softly. 'We're alike in that, you and I. Proud and guarded and too self-sufficient. I can understand all right.'

'As for running away——' her voice sank so that he had to lean close to hear her '——I thought you would be so disgusted that you would never want to see me again.'

'Disgusted?' Guy sounded shaken. 'My darling, why on earth?'

She leaned forward, her brow resting against his chest.

'They were so awful, those papers. They made me feel so dirty.'

He stroked her hair soothingly, though his hand shook. 'Yes, they were messy stuff. But they only reflect badly on the fools that wrote them. And even that was ten years ago. You can afford to forget it.'

She said in a drowned voice, 'But what about Laurel?

If Rose doesn't approve of me she won't let Laurel come and live with us. Laurel,' she added in a sudden access of memory, 'said Rose wouldn't have my name mentioned in the house.'

'Laurel,' said her fond brother on a sigh, 'wants beating. I am strongly tempted to employ an army of gaolers to keep her in order.' He gave her a gentle shake. 'Honestly, my darling, can't you recognise adolescent dramatics when you see them? Rose doesn't give a damn who I marry.'

'Oh,' said Robin, suddenly more hopeful.

'And as for the baggage coming to live with us, she would have to negotiate extremely carefully.'

'Oh,' said Robin again, sitting up and smoothing her hair.

He watched her, his smile a little strained. Eventually he said, 'Will you give me another chance, lover? Can we start again?'

A delicious warmth began to creep over Robin. She appeared to consider it, lashes lowered.

'I don't think one can ever start again,' she said dispassionately.

He flinched. She looked at him under her lashes.

'Besides, you've had all the chances you need.'

He registered that, quick as a cat, seizing her chin and forcing her face up so that their eyes met; hers were dancing.

'You may not go to bed with prickly ladies on a first date: what do you think I do? I'd never been to bed with anyone before, let alone fall into his arms at a touch. On,' she added with irony, 'every occasion that presented itself. No, no, Mr Gerrard. You don't need any more chances. You've taken full advantage of the ones you've had.'

As if not daring to believe it, Guy said, 'But I've hurt you, insulted you. All but forced you.' His eyes fell away from hers. 'I'm not proud of the way I treated you last time we met,' he said gruffly.

Robin leaned forward, slipping her hands insidiously under the open collar of his shirt until her palms lay flat against his skin. She savoured the sensation of muscle and bone and beating blood under her fingertips.

'And that, too, was mutual,' she said.

He pulled her against him then, his mouth seeking hers with an undisguised desperation that told her more than she had ever suspected, more than she had dared to hope in her wildest fantasies, of his need for her. She surrendered with delight.

When he raised his head he said breathlessly, laughing, 'So you'll marry me, sweetest of my enemies?'

Robin nodded.

'No more intransigence? No more suspicion? No more heart to hearts with my appalling sister?'

She gave a gurgle of laughter, 'Not as long as you keep reassuring me.'

His eyes were warm. 'Now how do I do that?'

She leaned forward and kissed him long and sensuously. 'You'll find a way,' she said with confidence.

Harlequin Presents

Coming Next Month

Available in October wherever paperback books are sold, or through Harlequin Reader Service:

In the U.S.
P.O. Box 1397
Buffalo, N.Y.
14240-1397

In Canada
P.O. Box 2800, Postal Station A
5170 Yonge Street
Willowdale, Ontario M2N 6J3

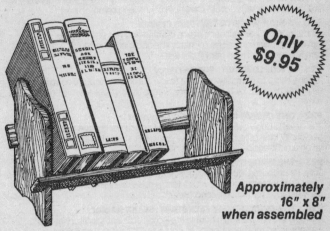

Could she find love as a mail-order bride?

MARIANNE WILLMAN

PIECES OF SKY

In the Arizona of 1873, Nora O'Shea is caught between life with a contemptuous, arrogant husband and her desperate love for Roger LeBeau, half-breed Comanche Indian scout and secret freedom fighter.

Available now at your favorite retail outlet, or order your copy by sending your name, address and zip or postal code along with a check or money order for $5.25 (includes 75¢ for postage and handling) payable to Worldwide Library Reader Service to:

In the U.S.

Worldwide Library
901 Fuhrmann Blvd.
Box 1325
Buffalo, New York
14269-1325

In Canada

Worldwide Library
P.O. Box 2800, 5170 Yonge St.
Postal Station A
Willowdale, Ontario
M2N 6J3

Please specify book title with your order.

 WORLDWIDE LIBRARY

SKYH-1R